A CLUTTER OF CATS

A CLUTTER OF CATS

A MAPLES MYSTERY

LOUISE CARSON

DOUG WHITEWAY, EDITOR

EDITIONS

Cover design by Doowah Design.
Cover icons courtesy of Noun Project.

This book was printed on Ancient Forest Friendly paper.
Printed and bound in Canada by Hignell Printing.

We acknowledge the support of the Canada Council for the Arts and the Manitoba Arts Council for our publishing program.

Library and Archives Canada Cataloguing in Publication

Title: A clutter of cats / Louise Carson ; Doug Whiteway, editor.
Names: Carson, Louise, 1957- author. | Whiteway, Doug- editor.
Description: Series statement: A Maples mystery

Identifiers: Canadiana (print) 20210327561 |
Canadiana (ebook) 2021032757X |
ISBN 9781773240923 (softcover) |
ISBN 9781773240930 (EPUB)

Classification: LCC PS8605.A7775 C58 2021 |
DDC C813/.6—dc23

Signature Editions
P.O. Box 206, RPO Corydon, Winnipeg, Manitoba, R3M 3S7
www.signature-editions.com

For Sandy,
and others who find themselves astray

CONTENTS

"A clowder of cats." 1801
(clowder var. cludder, clutter)

PART 1

DANGEROUS TO KNOW

M elancholy cried out. The flames were becoming hotter and hotter. No matter how small she made herself, there was no escaping them. She clawed at the sides of the metal barrel but they were slippery and she couldn't climb out.

She could hear the jeers of the drunken men who'd tossed her, some paper, and a book of lit matches into the barrel. She stretched as far up the side of the barrel as she could, screaming as she felt the flames burn her hind legs and tail.

She punched at the smooth circle of hot metal in which she was trapped but it was no good. It was too deep and too heavy to tip, and the fire was eating her.

Then there was a deluge of water, and steam and smoke choked her. "Oh, my God!" she heard a woman's voice say and a different voice, a man's, angry, saying, "I'm calling the police!" And then pain and silence and the dark.

The girl turned and twitched in her sleep, moved her feet, disturbing Melancholy, who woke, trembling. When the memories came to her, it was better if she was alone. She jumped off the bed and out of the room. The other cats on the girl's bed remained asleep.

Early morning. She would go outside. She slowly and awkwardly hopped down the stairs. The burned ligaments, muscles, tendons and even bone had healed, but she would never be flexible. She moved through the big room with the large table where many of the other cats were asleep. She didn't associate with them much.

She pushed against the square of carpet tacked over a small wall opening at the back of the room—the house's homemade cat flap. For three seasons' use only. She stepped out onto the narrow wooden deck, then down onto the flagstone path, both of which ran along the back of the house, and surveyed the day.

*Fine. Warm. Dry. She padded along the path, feeling the stones'
coolness, and paused near the girl's car, parked at the side of the
house. There was a garden shed the other side of the car and in front
of that, standing as close to the edge of the road as she could, was a
young woman in a long pink dress.*

*If Melancholy had cared at all about clothes she might have
noticed that the pink was a faded mauve, and that the details of the
dress—the piping around neck, bodice, sleeves and cuffs—were black.*

*As it was, she did notice that the woman was blonde and pale,
and that while her skirt moved as cars passed close, there was no
sound of flapping cloth.*

*The woman did nothing except turn her head first one way
then the other, looking first up the road where a small hill ascended,
then down where the road disappeared around a sharp curve.*

*Bored, Melancholy turned and descended the stone steps from
the parking pad to the lawn, keeping close to the shrubs and flower
beds that edged it. She entered the thicket beyond the flower beds
and paused, forgetting the woman.*

*Birds darted in and out of the newly leafed-out raspberry canes
and wild roses. Perhaps a bird would land agreeably close to her
nose and she—there—no—it fluttered out of reach. The stump of
her tail quivered. It had taken many months before she could trust
that its instinctive responses would no longer pain her. She felt her
tension release.*

*Beyond the thicket was the yard, partially overgrown, partially
lawn, of the large white house next door. A car pulled into the
driveway that circled behind it. A woman got out hurriedly, looking
furtively around her the way squirrels did when they left the safety
of trees for the ground. Melancholy could tell this woman was older
by the way she moved.*

*The woman opened one back door of the car, releasing her
big black dog. Melancholy stiffened until she saw the dog was on
its leash. The two entered the house, the woman reappearing alone*

holding some newspaper. She opened the trunk of her car, then stuffed something wrapped in the newspaper in the garbage can. The woman inspected her hands, then went back inside. The cat dozed.

She woke when she heard the sound of a bike arriving behind her at her own house. The cleaner. Then she heard the girl come out of the house, calling something to the cleaner. Melancholy turned to observe her current owner.

The girl had taken her coffee and sat at the picnic table on the lawn, staring at the lake. She sipped, making little mmming noises. The cat's stomach growled. She supposed she'd missed breakfast. The girl tossed her long hair back and sighed.

Melancholy turned her attention back to the house next door. The dog and woman had reappeared. This time the dog was off its leash and it trotted straight to the garbage can. The woman called it away.

1

Away they go cluttering like hey—go mad. (1759)[1]

"I often look through the thicket at the big white house next door and wonder about the lady who lives there."

The opening words to her Aunt Maggie's story "The Laughing Child" slid into Gerry's head as she watched her new neighbour and her black Labrador retriever loiter in their backyard. The woman seemed to be inspecting her garden, neglected for many years by her predecessor.

Gerry was not the ten-year-old girl from fifty years ago as her aunt had been, peering at the mysterious elderly lady next door and writing a curious little composition for school.

Gerry was a grown-up lady (ostensibly), though at the moment, crouching in the underbrush that separated the two properties, trying to unobtrusively coax the most difficult of her twenty cats back onto her property, she didn't feel very dignified— for all her twenty-six years.

Now that the house was occupied, and by a large dog as well as two people, she assumed her cats would not be welcome to slither through the brambles in search of excitement in its backyard. Besides, she'd seen the speed of the Labrador chasing

---

1   All epigraphs are from the *Oxford English Dictionary*.

squirrels. He hadn't caught any yet, but he'd come close. Neither she nor her cats needed that kind of excitement!

"Psst! Lightning!" Gerry tried to suck lips quietly—the traditional cat call—not that most of them bothered to respond unless she waved a treat in front of them. As she opened and closed her mouth goldfish style, she came out with an indistinct clicking sound.

The cat in question, a mostly black shorthaired tortoiseshell with an orange zigzag above her nose, glared. She would no doubt have been vigorously thrashing her tail, if she'd had one. As it was, her whole body quivered with tension. Fixating on Gerry, she seemed unaware of the canine threat behind her. Even though disaster seemed imminent, Gerry, an artist, couldn't help noticing how pretty Lightning looked, surrounded by the low clumps of purple violets that overran the thicket, tender green shrubbery above.

The neighbour wandered back toward her house, calling her pet. Her inspection must be over. Gerry took a step, a twig cracked, and the dog's head swung in their direction. Gerry and the two animals froze. Gerry sneezed. The dog gave a startled muted bark and began trotting towards them. Then it accelerated.

Gerry flung herself on Lightning. Thorns scratched her bare arms and nettles prickled her legs. She grasped the cat who grasped back. "Ahhhh!" breathed a by now well-punctured Gerry, still trying to be discreet.

The neighbour noticed the fracas—well, she could hardly not—and called her dog. "Shadow!" It stopped just short of the thicket. Its owner approached at a lope. For the first time, Gerry saw her new neighbour close up.

She was tall, late middle aged, with greying long brown hair tied back, and glasses. A permanent frown line furrowed her brow. She was dressed modestly but nicely in beige summer slacks, sandals and a white short-sleeved jersey. A necklace of chunky wooden beads completed the ensemble. She quickly leashed the dog and stared confusedly at Gerry who was holding a struggling Lightning above her head.

"Oh, hello." Gerry tried to sound nonchalant. "My cat was wandering onto your property and I was trying to get it back. Onto my property." She lowered the cat, turned and released her. Lightning shot back into Gerry's yard, disappearing from view. The dog whined and strained at its leash.

His owner jerked the plaited leather and said, "Hush, Shadow."

Gerry carefully picked her way through the shrubbery toward them and stuck out her hand. "I'm Gerry Coneybear. Welcome to the neighbourhood."

The woman looked at the somewhat grimy and newly bloodied hand. She repressed a shudder. "I won't shake, if you don't mind. I'm going out in a moment."

Gerry withdrew the hand and grinned. "Sorry. I was pulling a few weeds. That's when I noticed the cat was over here. Good thing for us your dog is so well—"

She'd been going to say trained but evidently the woman had decided to be sociable, for she interrupted Gerry with "I'm Edwina Murray. And this is Shadow."

Gerry bent over. The dog sat. "Hello, Shadow. Pleased to meet you. Catch any squirrels yet?"

He looked at her with his intelligent brown eyes. Edwina spoke for him. "Not yet. Not here, anyway. But he keeps trying. Barks at them from inside the house. Most annoying. Actually," and here she looked around her vaguely as if seeking someone. "Actually, he belongs more to my husband, Roald."

Gerry had seen the husband, a large fleshy man with a red face, arguing with one of the tradesmen who'd been working on the house for several months. "Oh, yes? May I pet Shadow? I love dogs." When Edwina nodded, Gerry crouched next to the dog. "Who's a good boy?" she crooned as she scratched his head.

The dog closed his eyes. His tongue lolled out of his mouth. He panted slowly.

"I see you do. Yet you have cats." She said this somewhat accusingly.

Gerry stood up. "It's a long story. Basically, I inherited them. From my aunt. Along with the house. Like you." She stopped in some confusion, not wanting to seem curious, though she was.

Edwina merely nodded. "That's right. My great-aunt, actually. Or maybe she was a cousin. A great-cousin. I'm not sure. Two generations separated us so it's hard to say. My great-grandmother was Helen Parsley, the original owner of the house with her husband, and my Aunt Winnifred's mother. Winnifred didn't have any children." She added matter-of-factly, "Like me. Well, I do have an appointment."

"You must come for tea one day," Gerry offered.

"Tea?" Edwina seemed confused by the invitation then collected herself. "Yes. Tea. That would be nice. Goodbye for now."

Thinking that tea and lunch sounded like a very good idea, Gerry retreated to her own house. But first, she paused on the parking pad next to the side kitchen entrance and gazed at the view.

For over two hundred years The Maples, family home of the Coneybears for many generations, had stood, its back to the road to Lovering, surveying that other, older road, the waterway that was the Lake of Two Mountains, as this part of the Ottawa River was called. The building rambled away to her right, yellow with white trim, its formal garden showing tulips, daffodils and other spring flowers of which Gerry was still ignorant.

The property's lawn, speckled with little white wild violets, sloped gently to the wildflower garden, not yet in flower, then to a pebbly beach and shore. A green canoe was drawn up there.

The lake itself, on this beautiful mid-May day, shone blue-grey, its dimpled surface moving only slightly, while on the opposite shore, a pine forest steadfastly separated lake from sky. Word of Lightning's close call must have spread through the feline community, for none of its members was visible on Gerry's property.

Gerry took a deep breath of contentment and went inside. Her tiny kitchen's tidiness was only marred by the evidence of the cats' breakfasts. Twenty little saucers were drying in the dish rack. From upstairs she heard the sound of the vacuum. She checked the time. Noon. Time for her and Prudence to have their lunches. Time for Prudence to have a break from the never-ending task of keeping Gerry from wading knee-deep in cat fur. She put on the kettle and reached for a giant tin of Scottish shortbread, not without some guilt at not having baked for over a week. "Dang it all!" she protested to herself. "I'm on holiday!"

She'd had a burst of energy and creativity that month, had had a weekend garage sale that had considerably emptied out her shed of its odds and ends of old furniture and tools, and managed to get ten extra days' worth of her comic strip *Mug the Bug* done. As she'd already had another ten strips filed, that meant she could take the next two, three or even four weeks off. She smiled in happy anticipation.

No *Mug*. No art class to teach. No deadlines of any kind. No *Dibble* to market. And money in the bank.

Dibble was her self-published children's book *The Cake-Jumping Cats of Dibble*, and the art class was just a little one she gave at the house to a few locals. The people of Lovering scattered in the summer; some to distant cottages or foreign destinations (though why one would want to leave Lovering in the summer, the one season everyone waited for through the six-month-long winters, Gerry couldn't figure out); and some to pursue outdoor activities like playing golf and tennis, though gardening was the one hobby many of Lovering's inhabitants held in common. She wondered if her new neighbour was a gardener. She'd have her work cut out for her, if so.

Gerry herself had decided to get her hands dirty this summer and found she quite enjoyed it. She'd had no idea how relaxing weeding and moving perennials around could be.

The vacuum cleaner noise ceased. Gerry opened the kitchen door. "Prudence! Lunch break! I'm making tea." She waited.

"All right," came the distant answer.

Gerry closed the door. She poured a bit of boiling water in the brown teapot to warm it, then swooshed it around before pouring it down the sink. She took a mason jar of tea out of the cupboard. The tea was a new flavour, Earl Grey Cream, superior, Gerry thought, to the traditional Earl Grey, and a gift from a friend. She packed three teaspoons of the leaves into a vintage white china tea egg and carefully screwed it closed. One of her Aunt Maggie's cherished possessions.

Another of the cherished possessions scratched at the kitchen door. "All right! All right! I'm coming!" she called, adding fresh boiling water to the pot and loading it along with all necessary tea accoutrements onto a big round tray. No cats in the kitchen was the almost always strictly enforced (except at cat meal times) rule.

The waiting cat was Seymour, the newest addition to Gerry's feline family and one of the cats who had *not* belonged to her aunt. A small black shorthair, he was usually a polite gentleman. The previously rescued tortoiseshell, Lightning, hovered nervously in the background. "What's up, Seymour?" Gerry queried, placing the tray down on the big table by the lakeside window.

Then she forgot the two cats as, once again entranced by the view, she looked dreamily out the window.

In fall, winter and early spring, she would probably have set her and Prudence's tea tray on the little table between the two rockers facing the fire, but now it was summer (well, practically), Gerry couldn't get enough of her backyard view: green lawn, though brown or yellow in patches; flowers poking up; and the trees, mostly maples, soft with partially opened leaves. She picked Seymour up and absently stroked him. As only the second of her cats that she'd selected herself (the first being the kitten Jay from a batch of five brought home by her motherly marmalade tabby Mother) she had a special spot in her heart for him. She looked at his little face, slightly disfigured by the absence of one eye. "Who's a lovely boy?" she crooned, rubbing her face in his fur. He purred and pushed his head against her chin, seeming to say, "That would be me." She sneezed. Disturbed by the sudden violent sound, the cat jumped down.

"Sounds like someone's got allergies," commented Prudence, going into the kitchen to get her lunch, a peanut butter and sweet pickle sandwich with accompanying bag of potato chips.

Today's flavour was vinegar. She offered the open bag to Gerry as she sat down at the table. Gerry took one and got her own already prepared chicken sandwich from the fridge.

Various cats, hearing sounds of snacking, sidled or stalked (depending on their character) into the room and ranged themselves comfortably around the seated pair—the young woman with red hair and freckles, and the older woman, grey hair pulled back in a bun, her small mouth pursed.

A big marmalade (Mother) corralled a small black and white cat (Jay), and, holding it firmly between its front paws, began a thorough grooming. The black and white cat squirmed as another small cat (Ronald)—white with a black moustache—strolled by, smirking. "We've all had to put up with it," he might have been saying.

He joined three grey-striped cats who were flipping and flopping on the braided hearthrug, using each other's tails as toys. A large tuxedo cat sat nearby, licking a paw.

"I don't *think* I do," sniffled Gerry, blowing her nose, "but I have been congested for a few days. I thought a spring cold, but I don't feel sick."

"Look at your eyes, all puffed up." Prudence, having finished her lunch, reached for a shortbread. Real imported Scottish shortbread was about the only non-home-baked dessert Prudence would concede *might* be almost as good as her own killer version. (The secret ingredient is rice flour, which she grinds herself, but that's another story.) "Is the tea brewed?"

Gerry yawned as she poured a clear liquid into one of the teacups.

"Hoo boy," sighed Prudence, rising. "Allergies'll do that to you. Make you kind of dopey and sleepy." She took the hot-water filled pot and emptied it into the sink, before putting the kettle on to reboil and checking that the tea egg on the counter actually contained tea.

"But I never had them in Toronto," wailed Gerry, who'd spent the first twenty-five years of her life there before coming to Lovering the year before. "And I was here last spring and nothing happened."

"You were here briefly for Maggie's funeral in late May, then didn't get back until, what? Mid-, late June? After you packed up and moved." The kettle whistled and this time tea was included in the ceremony. Prudence set the cozy-covered pot on the tray in front of Gerry. Fittingly, given the shortbread they were eating, the cozy was white with botanical drawings of the flowers of Scotland on it: yellow gorse and broom alternated with purple heather and thistle.

"The main tree-pollen season would have been over by then."

"You're right. I am absent-minded. I forgot the cozy as well as the tea." Gerry pressed the heels of her palms to her eyes. "Oh, that feels good. I have a headache too."

"Allergies," confirmed Prudence. "See the doc."

"Why not just buy something at the drugstore?"

"You want something that *works*, don't you?" her friend replied, witheringly critical of all over-the-counter drugs other than aspirin. "What are you going to do with your week off?"

"Two weeks," Gerry corrected. "Maybe three. Even four if I get deep into relaxation mode." She added gloomily, "And you mean, other than have allergies."

"Oh, go make an appointment now!"

An increasingly sniffy Gerry did. When she returned from her call to the doctor's office she found Prudence had poured them each a fragrant cup of Earl Grey. Gerry sighed, leaned back and closed her eyes. "What will I do? I don't know. Just be, maybe? Not rush. Breathe." She sneezed hugely, jarring the more nervous of her cats. Even Bob the tuxedo cat, he of the steady temperament, paused in his grooming. "Sorry, Bob." He blinked lazily. He didn't *look* bothered.

"When's your appointment?" asked Prudence, swiftly moving the open tin of shortbreads out of sneeze range.

"Eleven-thirty tomorrow," mumbled Gerry.

"Huh. You were lucky. Bring something to read. You'll wait at least an hour. Meanwhile, have another cup of tea. You should flush your system."

"Yes, Prudence. Anything you say, Prudence," Gerry acquiesced, eyes twinkling, in what she hoped was an annoying manner.

Prudence changed the subject by picking up a copy of *Dibble*. "Don't you need to order more of these? I remember you telling me you were down to your last ten."

"No, I don't. I finally heard from the agent. Or manager. Publicist? Whatever she is. She's agreed to take over the marketing for *Dibble*, for a percentage, of course. From my cut, not the charity's," she hastily added. *Dibble*'s profits, meagre though they were, were shared with a local cat rescue and adoption agency CRAS (Cat Rescue Adoption Society). The same one where she'd found Seymour.

Prudence nodded. "That's good. You could hardly keep driving from one vet's office to another. Or pet food stores."

"Yeah. Very time consuming. But you know, when they heard it was for a cat rescue society, they all gave the book counter space. Denise, that's the agent—or is she a distributor?" She frowned. Prudence rolled her eyes and Gerry laughed. "Denise had one good idea already. She's arranged for the next printing of *Dibble* to include the words 'Creator of *Mug the Bug*' after my name on the front and back covers."

Prudence nodded. "Smart. Still, books belong in bookstores." Then she gently chided, "And you don't need to hustle like you've been doing. Now the painting's finally properly sold."

She was referring to Gerry's other inheritance. Besides the cats, the house and a small amount of cash to help maintain them, Aunt Maggie had left, among her collection of family portraits and "nice" landscapes by local painters, one valuable object—a small oil painting by the acclaimed mid-twentieth-century Quebec artist Paul-Émile Borduas.

After many false starts and one giant misappropriation, the untitled work had finally sold (through Gerry's and Prudence's mutual friend Bertie Smith, antique and art dealer) and Gerry had been paid. The many, many thousands of dollars had been carefully invested in various certificates, all timed to release interest over the subsequent years, and some capital should it be needed.

At the thought of all that future financial security nestled in the bank, Gerry relaxed. "You know, I think I'm going to just do nothing for the next few weeks. Oh, before I forget. I found out the new neighbour's name. It's Edwina Murray. Her husband's name is Roald but he wasn't there. I've invited her to tea sometime." She took in her friend's astonished face. "What!?"

Prudence's eyes were wide. She put down her cup. "*The* Edwina Murray?"

"I don't know. Is there a special one?"

"You know: the mystery author! Wrote *Dangerous to Know*; *Home to Roost*; *Purple Angel*. Is it her?"

"Er, she didn't say—"

"What does she look like?"

"Ah, about your age. Taller, thin, wears a ponytail, glasses."

"Oh. My. God. That's got to be her. She is one of my favourite authors. Her mysteries are very dark."

"Well, you must come to tea when she does. And right now— " She stood and drained her cup. "I am going for a nap. You're right, allergies do make you sleepy. But I'll get up later and drive you home."

"No need. I'm on my bike, remember? I'll finish up and be off shortly. See you Thursday."

"See you Thursday," Gerry replied thickly, relieved that now the fine weather had arrived and, more importantly, the masses of snow that narrowed Lovering's already narrow streets in winter had melted away, Prudence, who was only now in her fifties learning how to drive, could find her own way to and from work without needing lifts from Gerry. She stumbled up the stairs to her room and collapsed on the bed. She fell into a deep sleep.

She was on the lake, paddling in the green canoe. It was very quiet and she couldn't tell the time of day because a thick fog enveloped her. The water was still, and drops from the tip of her upraised paddle fell back onto the surface, making tiny indentations. But there were so many drops, so many indentations. She realized that it must be raining.

It was strange. She didn't feel wet. The fog seemed to be keeping her dry. She opened her eyes and realized she was warm in her bed with the sheet pulled over her head. She heard the sound of a light rain on the metal roof above her bedroom. "Naps!" she exclaimed to Seymour and Lightning, Seymour curled into her belly, Lightning at her feet. "They can be disorienting."

The cats, who, being cats, probably enjoyed about ten or twenty naps per day, merely blinked inscrutably.

"To wake is human, to nap—feline," murmured Gerry, feeling she was vaguely paraphrasing someone's more profound previous utterance. She grabbed Seymour's paw and gave it a playful shake. "Who said that, Seymour? Was it you? Was it?"

Seymour, a shy little fellow but always up for a quiet game, responded by batting at her hand. Gerry sat up and reached for a tissue. Her stuffy nose and watering sore eyes, temporarily relieved by her nap, had returned. She sneezed and blew, then went rigid with horror.

"What if I'm allergic to cats?" she cried. Only the raindrops, gently beating on the roof, replied.

2

Impossible to have found so little a thing, in so great
a clutter of thick, and deep Grass. (1674)

Gerry put down the book she was reading with a sigh. Finished. *Swallows and Amazons* by Arthur Ransome. A children's book but entertaining, full of holidays on a lake in northern England spent camping and sailing and having adventures. She sometimes felt being an only child had robbed her of these kinds of experiences. She'd never had a sibling she could go off with, so had been kept close to her parents.

She turned to the flyleaf. Gerry Coneybear, it said in her late father's handwriting. From when *he'd* been a boy. She'd found the book and the eleven others in the series in a bookcase in her aunt's special bamboo room, a retreat at the far end of the house full of art and books and precious objects, not least of which was the bamboo wall lining.

She promised herself a glorious few weeks of reading the other books. But meanwhile…

Prudence had been right. It was 12:30, over an hour past her scheduled appointment. She glanced around the doctor's waiting room, obviously furnished with cast-offs from the doctor's home—a sofa, some comfy armchairs, and stacks of old *National Geographic* and *Mad* magazines.

Gerry didn't really enjoy *Mad* but as a cartoonist it engaged her. She picked up a copy.

"Miss Coneybear?" The doctor, a small woman about Gerry's height, stood at the door of her office. She smiled warmly.

"Nice to meet you, Dr. Barron," Gerry said.

"Likewise. Sorry to keep you waiting. Are you here for—ah, here it is." She consulted her notes. "You think you have allergies. Why? What are your symptoms?"

By way of an answer Gerry coughed, sniffed, sneezed and blew her nose all in a few seconds.

Dr. Barron smiled. "Hmm. I see. And you don't think you have a cold?" Gerry shook her head. "And are you allergic to anything else you already know about?" Again Gerry shook her head. The doctor continued, "Any pets? A lot of dust in your home? Do you garden?"

"Yes, no, and yes," Gerry replied, feeling sheepish. "Twenty cats, which is why the house is professionally cleaned twice a week." She continued, rather desperately, "But I've lived there for a year and this is the first time—"

Dr. Barron interrupted her. "And you garden?"

"Yes. That's new. My housekeeper—perhaps you know her?—Prudence Crick?" The doctor nodded. "She says it's probably tree pollen. All the little catkins, on the trees, I mean, opening and dropping pollen everywhere..." She trailed off, her eyes at the mention of pollen watering uncontrollably. "And I'm awfully sleepy."

"I see," said the doctor, and made a note. "You know, sometimes allergies take a while to show up. So it might be the cats." At Gerry's look of distress, she held up her hand. "But your friend might be right. It is spring allergy season. Let's assume it's that. For now. Do you take any medication? No? And I'll need a pee sample, please." She handed Gerry the little container.

After a few more questions, Gerry left with a prescription for a nasal spray and tablet, and a strong feeling of liking for her new doctor. "Kind and sensible," she muttered, as she drove to the pharmacy. "Like Prudence." She thought about the year Prudence had had.

Where Gerry had lost an aunt she didn't know very well and hadn't seen in years, Prudence had lost her best friend. Prudence had found Maggie's body and Prudence, along with Gerry, had kept the secret that the death was a result of murder for almost a year before revealing the identity of the guilty person.

And Prudence had already been struggling with the not-so-recent loss of her mother, and still employed one Mrs. Smith, a perfectly nice woman Gerry had met, as a psychic, to help Prudence communicate with her mother's spirit.

And then, when, the previous Christmas, a super storm had sent a tree onto the roof of Gerry's shed and car, the same storm had seen half of Prudence's little cottage crushed, also by a tree, and she'd had to shelter with Gerry and others for months.

After that, Prudence's husband, Alexander Crick, had finished serving a long sentence for bank robbery with violence, and made brief contact with Prudence before he got out. His original crime had resonated down the years to such effect that another murder had occurred. Prudence had to see to the aftermath of all that with the dredging up of mostly bad memories from her youth.

Kind and sensible and tough, mused Gerry, pulling into the pharmacy parking lot. Very tough.

Speaking of tough, she thought, as she caught sight of the woman sitting waiting for a prescription, there's my other aunt. The live one.

Though Aunt Mary's hair was carefully tinted and coiffed, her face betrayed her age. Under the makeup, Gerry thought she could see new lines on the sixty-something face. She looks thinner, she thought. She pushed her prescription through the wicket at the smiling assistant, then took a seat next to the woman. "Hello, Aunt Mary," she said carefully, unsure of her aunt's reaction.

Her aunt looked straight ahead. "Gerry," she replied.

Gerry turned her body, noting the arm in a sling. "Aunt Mary, I wish—"

"Mrs. Petherbridge?" called the assistant.

Gerry jumped up, supporting her aunt by her good arm. To her surprise, her assistance was accepted. Her aunt received quite a few medications. Gerry sneezed.

"I hope you're not going to give me a cold!" Mary snapped.

Gerry grinned. This was more like it. "No. Allergies."

She received and paid for her own prescriptions and realized, again to her surprise, that her aunt seemed to be loitering. As if she *wanted* to speak to Gerry—Gerry, who'd inherited the family home from Mary's sister Maggie, when all along, Mary had expected to be the beneficiary. This had led to some resentment on Mary's part, and Gerry knew that her cousin Margaret's motivation to do bad things had come from her mother's openly vented discontent, as well as a lifetime of maternal neglect.

Together they slowly walked to the exit. "I'm glad—" "I meant—" "No, you," they said at the same time. Gerry indicated her aunt should speak first.

Mary cleared her throat as Gerry held the door open for her. "I meant to thank you for the flowers you sent while I was—" Mary paused as if searching for a way to describe recovering in hospital from being attacked in her home with a knife by her only daughter. They stood outside the store.

Gerry finished her sentence for her: "—while you were recuperating. I asked Andrew what your favourites were and he said yellow roses, so—I was going to say I'm glad you're out and about." She walked her aunt to her large expensive car. "And I'm glad the insurance company finally paid out Uncle Geoff's life insurance." Gerry had learned this from Andrew, Mary and Geoff's son, Gerry's cousin, who'd been much relieved at the payout, as since his father's death, he'd been giving his mother money to help her maintain her big house and upper middle-class lifestyle.

Mary clicked the key fob to unlock the doors. "Well, the wounds were superficial. She didn't—" She seemed to choke on the words. "Margaret didn't actually stab me. If she had, I'd probably be—"

Both women were silent, contemplating the horrific scene the night Margaret had injured her mother. Gerry had seen the trashed kitchen where Margaret had gone wild, and in Mary's bedroom where Margaret had finally dropped the carving knife and knelt, keening, next to her unconscious mother, the blood. In Gerry's opinion, Mary was lucky to be alive.

Mary slid carefully behind the steering wheel. "Andrew's been very kind to me."

"He's kind to everyone, as far as I can see. You raised him well."

Mary grunted. "I don't suppose…" she began diffidently.

"Shall I come to you or would you like to come to The Maples? How about tea? I'd be happy to make you scones. Perhaps with clotted cream and some of Prudence's excellent strawberry jam?" Gerry's voice sounded hopeful in her own ears. She touched her aunt's shoulder. "After all, you are my last Coneybear aunt," she said quietly.

Mary nodded and turned the key. "It would be nice to see the old place again."

"I'll call you," Gerry said as her aunt reversed the car. Gerry sat in her own car for a moment. She took a big breath and forcefully blew it out. "Whew! Wow!" She blew her nose and drove home.

After she'd made herself a ham and cheese sandwich and eaten it, and as she was savouring a vanilla hazelnut coffee on the back porch, she realized, with no work schedule, she really didn't have a clue what to do. There's always the garden, she thought, contemplating its many beds. But where to start?

She changed into her gardening clothes (dark blue sweatpants, one of her boyfriend Doug's long-sleeved flannel shirts and a big floppy straw hat she'd found in the gardening shed) and wandered onto the parking pad. Bob, her large tuxedo cat, followed her, trailed by Seymour and, at a distance, Lightning. Other cats fooled around under shrubs and at the edges of the lawn. The kitten Jay, who was enjoying her first spring, foolishly paused in the middle of the yard. Swallows, nesting under the eaves of the house, began to dive bomb her. She immediately sagged low to the ground and trotted to join the cats who were with Gerry. Gerry bet the other cats were thinking, "You can only learn from experience."

"I'll begin on my left and work my way around," she announced to her little gang. As she descended the stone steps to the lawn, she took in the full beauty of mid-spring. Arguably the best month of the year, May, she thought. No mosquitoes yet. Cool at night so good for sleeping.

She followed the arc where lawn met thicket and glanced at the house next door. The busy refurbishment by its new owners seemed to have died down—there was only one trades' van in the driveway.

Edwina Murray came out of her back door and stood, rather irresolutely, it seemed to Gerry, and stared at the lake. Gerry waved and Edwina approached her side of the thicket.

"Lovely day," called Gerry. Soft pressure at ankle height made her look down. Both Seymour and Lightning were twined around her lower legs. That's funny, one part of Gerry's brain noted, even as the other part made chit-chat with Edwina, who, it transpired, was taking a breather from writing her latest novel.

"I'm not sure if the murderer *is* the murderer. Do you see?" Through her glasses, she peered vaguely at Gerry, as if hoping she'd provide the answer.

As both Seymour and Lightning were trying to climb Gerry's legs, Gerry's attention wandered.

"It's called *The Case Against—*"

"Ah ha ha ha ha!" interrupted Gerry, bending down to detach first one, then the other of her weirdly behaving pets, who promptly darted away towards the gardening shed at the front of the property. Bob, watching all of this, looked from Edwina to Gerry, then departed as well.

"I'm so sorry," gasped Gerry, rubbing her legs, "I wasn't paying attention." But neither, it seemed, was Edwina, who wandered away, muttering.

"Sorry about that," Gerry called after her. "Come to tea on Thursday. Three-ish." She took the wave Edwina made behind her retreating back to signal a yes and resumed her backyard patrol, a little the worse for wear. Fortunately, the pants were thick, so she was only slightly damaged.

She paused before the rhubarb. Something about pie, she remembered. Had Aunt Maggie made rhubarb pie one summer vacation when Gerry was very little? She remembered someone handing her a stalk raw from the plant and her mouth puckering at the acid taste. The plant was huge.

"How much pie did people used to eat?" she asked Bob, who sat delicately under one enormous leaf, regarding her gravely with his golden eyes. "Cat umbrella," she murmured dreamily, and "I'm as bad as Edwina." She smiled when she remembered what Prudence had said the day before. "We have to keep on top of the rhubarb."

Then, Gerry's cartoonist's eye had pictured Prudence lying on top of the rhubarb, possibly with a quizzical cat or two nearby. "You're picturing me on top of the rhubarb, aren't you?" a sour-faced Prudence had guessed. Gerry had snickered.

After the rhubarb, stuck for some reason all by itself away from the main garden, there were only wild flowers until the lawn petered out and the rocky beach began.

As the wild flowers were still just a mass of greenery, the only weeds Gerry felt safe enough to pull were grasses. She busied herself for a few minutes, then got bored and sauntered along the lake side of her property, looking at the view.

She heard birds and squirrels, a small boat's motor as it putted downriver and—a cat mewing. A cat mewing frantically. She ran towards the sound.

In a cedar-hedge-enclosed area the land rose from beach level and here was an ancient empty swimming pool, surrounded by a white picket fence. Doug had drained it in the fall to make repairs. Gerry opened the gate and rushed to the pool.

Mother paced back and forth at one side. It was her mewing Gerry had heard, for inside the pool, sniffing dead leaves and twigs in apparent unconcern, was Mother's latest adopted child, half-grown Jay.

Gerry relaxed. "It's okay, Mother. Jay's all right. She must have landed on leaves. I'll get a ladder." Five minutes later, Gerry ascended the ladder and turned Jay over to Mother, who began a head-to-tail inventory of her charge's parts.

Everything seemed in order and Gerry watched from the top of the ladder as Jay scampered off. Bob, Lightning and Seymour, as well as other cats drawn by the commotion, now clustered about the pool edges.

"Now, nobody else fall in," admonished Gerry. After eying the mass of dead tree material in the pool, she fetched a rake and some big paper bags, which she tossed in. "Who wants to come investigate?" Only Bob came close enough to be grabbed. With him perched on her shoulder, she descended back into the pool.

Gerry hummed quietly to herself while Bob pounced on every leaf pile she raked. "You were a mistake," she accused and shook a finger. Nonplussed, he began burrowing in one of the tantalizing, rustling mounds.

Tired, she sat on another pile and looked up. It was odd to be at the bottom of the pool instead of floating on its surface. The giant willow and mature maples were not yet fully in leaf. Some of her cats were still watching from above: the grey-striped trio known as the boys—Winston, Franklin and Joseph—and their sidekick Ronald, he of the white fur and little black moustache. The rest of the pride had scattered. She wondered when she could safely fill the pool. The frost-free date must be soon.

Gerry heard Bob give a little clucking cry and dropped her gaze. "Eeeeeee!" Bob froze, then resumed dragging bits of dead bird—long dead bird—out from their place of interment in one of the piles. "No! Bobbeee! Yuck!" She sprang to remove the bits, but, wing in mouth, Bob trotted to the foot of the ladder.

"I'll compromise," said Gerry. "You can have the wing. But don't throw up all over my bedroom carpet tonight!" She carried Bob and his trophy up to the edge of the pool. He flattened his ears and made weird threatening noises in his throat as other cats tried to investigate. Then he trotted furtively under a cedar and began to dismantle the wing. "Cats!" she snorted in disgust and returned to her task.

As she dropped the last rakeful of leaves into the last bag, something glinted in the sun as it fell with a small clank onto the pool's concrete floor.

Gerry hung the phone back on its receiver on the kitchen wall. Well, that hadn't been so bad, she thought. She'd invited Aunt Mary to tea on Thursday. Now to tell Prudence. She dialled.

"Hello?"

"Hi, Prudence, it's me. How are you?"

"Fine. What's up?"

"Well, I thought you'd like to know who's coming to tea on Thursday."

"Oh yes." Prudence sounded wary.

"Do you want the good news first or the bad?"

"Bad."

"I met Aunt Mary at the drugstore and she seemed really changed, Prudence." Gerry heard a kind of growl at the other end of the line. Prudence had little time for Mary, who had always treated her like a "lowly" servant, mocked her simple lifestyle and hadn't seemed to grieve (as Prudence had) when Mary's only sister—Maggie—had died. "No, really. All kind of exhausted. Too exhausted to be nasty." Gerry waited for a further reaction, then spoke into the silence. "So I invited her to tea. With scones."

"Hmm. Your house," was Prudence's reply.

"Yeah. And now for the good news. Your author—Edwina Murray—is coming as well. I told Aunt Mary to come at 2:30 and Edwina to come at three. Okay?"

"Way to ruin a wonderful opportunity to meet someone I really admire," Prudence said.

"Well, that's telling me," Gerry said flatly. "I *think* Mary will be good. That's why I invited her to come early. If she's rude, we'll just chuck her out."

But Prudence had forgotten Mary. "I'll bake a cake for Edwina. Scones aren't enough. And we're making jam."

"We are?"

"Gotta keep on top of the rhubarb," Prudence predictably said. Gerry smirked but said nothing. "You buy a bag of sugar, a couple of lemons and a small piece of whole ginger root." Prudence seemed to be thinking aloud. "I know you have jars somewhere."

"All right. Wait a minute. I'm writing it down. I'll look for jars."

"I think they're in boxes way back at either end of the lower kitchen cupboards."

"Got it." There was a pause. "I think it'll be fine, Prudence. I really do. Mary is usually charming with strangers."

"I hope you're right. Anyway, as I said, your house." She changed the subject. "Did you see the doctor?"

"Yes. She gave me a couple of prescriptions."

"And? Are they working?"

"Wait a second." They waited. "Why, I believe they are. That's great. I was working outside and holding Jay and Bob but my sniffles are almost completely gone."

"She's a good doctor."

"Yes. In fact, she phoned this morning. Wants me to have a blood test."

"Oh?"

"Yeah. As I'm a new patient she's 'working up my profile' was how she described it. All right then. See you soon."

Gerry prepared the twenty little dishes, each with a spoonful of tinned cat meat, put them on the floor and opened the kitchen door. The hairy mob streamed in, some gobbling their meat right away, others crunching at the footbath-sized tub of kibble under the kitchen table. Of course this meant that some cats received more than one serving of meat, but it all worked out in the end. Maybe some of them preferred the kibble.

She found the boxes of jam jars where Prudence had said they might be and stacked them in a corner of the room. Then she took her coffee and a couple of shortbreads onto the back porch with the second volume of the Swallows and Amazons adventure books—*Swallowdale*. She propped her feet on a rickety cushioned wicker footstool and relaxed.

After a few chapters in which an accident with one of their sailboats marooned some of the children and they discovered a cave as part of one of the world's best camping places, she paused and looked up. Tomorrow she would return to weeding.

She reached into her pants pocket and retrieved the gold wedding band she'd found in the pool. No marks, no inscription. She slipped it on.

"Marry me?" he murmured and kissed her neck. A raucous "caw, caw" roused her from *that* daydream. A crow—or was it a raven—something about the shape of the tail was supposed to distinguish one from the other—anyway, a large black bird sat on a bough of the willow that overhung the pool. Gerry watched as it rocked back and forth, cawing.

She noticed the songbirds had quietened, except for one male sparrow that couldn't contain his springtime joy. Or longing. A different crow swooped from somewhere and took him, ending his song, and disappearing high into one of Edwina's trees. The other crow followed. She shuddered. Poor guy, she thought. But crows must eat. Then she returned the ring to her pocket, reopened her book and forgot all about it.

3

The world or whole clutter of bodies. (1674)

Gerry's boyfriend, Doug Shapland, was away camping with his grown-up sons: James, Geoff Jr. and David. They'd gone all the way to Algonquin Park in Ontario, a five-hour drive. Gerry hadn't liked to butt in by offering to accompany them. Let it be a bonding experience for father and sons. One way or another, they'd recently been through hard times, the mental illness of the boys' mother (Margaret, Doug's ex-wife) having reached a crisis when she'd attacked *her* mother, Mary.

So that evening she felt at a loose end. No work, no boyfriend. Her other friends were busy. This is what lonely people who don't have any interests feel like, she thought. She moped.

One of the longhaired cats, a grey and white named Cocoon, walked by, tufts of fur dangling. Gerry brightened. "I know! I'll groom the cats!" She retrieved her basket of combs, brushes and nail clippers and set to it.

About half of her clients were compliant. The elderly ones like Cocoon, Min Min, Harley and Kitty Cat; and those placid by nature like Mother, Mouse, Blackie, Whitey and Runt, let her brush them pretty thoroughly and clip their nails.

Bob (her favourite, it must be confessed, though she knew she shouldn't have a favourite) didn't like the nail clipping part, jerking his paw away after every nail.

By the time these "easy" cats were groomed, Gerry was trying to think of something else to do. Now for the high-energy cats. "Grit your teeth, girl," she encouraged herself, catching Jay (her other favourite, raised from a mewling weeks-old kitten) as she streaked by.

She wrapped Jay in a towel so as not to get scratched, and clipped cautiously as the little thing struggled. Then she gave Ronald the same treatment.

The boys were not so simple to trap. By scattering a line of cat treats on the floor, which attracted everyone, she was able to pick them off one by one, and take each towel-wrapped struggling captive into the privacy of the kitchen.

She found Max, a fluffy white and marmalade whose fur was prone to matting, in the dining room, along with Monkey, a shorthaired grey tiger stripe, sister to the boys, but without the deviltry. Jinx, a pretty longhaired grey with a white bib, she retrieved from the garden.

Gerry paused and counted cats who'd been groomed. Two missing. Seymour she didn't mind doing. He was gentle. But she groaned when she realized who else was left. Lightning. Both cats were shorthairs but she knew Lightning would never let her clip her claws. *Maybe when Doug gets back he can help me. And we'll wrap him in a really thick towel as well as the cat.* She yawned and went up to bed.

Four cats usually slept with her. Bob, her Top Cat, began the night snuggled either to Gerry's belly or back but often, on waking, could be found stretched out on her bedside rug. Jay, her little kitten, that winter had developed a fondness for draping herself along the top of Gerry's head where it rested on the pillow. (*My little cat hat* was one way Gerry described her.) Lightning, her most challenging pet, slept at her feet, closest to the door in case she had to make a quick getaway. And Seymour, the newest addition to the pride, jostled with Bob for the coveted belly or back positions.

When Gerry fell asleep this night, only Bob and Jay were with her. She drifted off, remembering Lightning and Seymour hanging around together, and thinking, that's nice, Lightning finally made a friend. When she awoke in the morning, all four cats were snugly in place, but Seymour was at the foot of her bed with his paws wrapped firmly about Lightning's neck.

Gerry flumped downstairs. "Not a morning person," she announced to the assembling cats, hungry for their breakfasts. She knew they didn't care. She shut herself in the kitchen to do the necessary chores, which included making a double espresso and frothing some hot milk. She opened the kitchen door, stepping over the entering cats and, still in pyjamas, robe and slippers, made her way to the screened back porch which to her was one of the house's chief delights.

Located behind a discreet door tucked to the rear of the grand entranceway at the centre of the house, which featured a wide galleried staircase and east-facing upstairs windows illuminating the area this morning, was the porch. It could not have provided a greater contrast to the interior.

A small square space with a painted wooden floor, and screened on three sides, its roof was covered in ivy. Ivy that was sprouting new leaves. In another few weeks, the porch would be a shady retreat.

Today, she felt a little coolness around her lower legs. Otherwise, it promised to be a perfect day.

The first sip of coffee was beginning to restore her faculties when the phone rang. "Rats!" She returned to the kitchen. "Hello?"

"Gerry! What a beautiful day!" It was Bea Muxworthy, one of Gerry's best friends.

"Hi, Bea," a less-than-enthusiastic Gerry mumbled. "Haven't had my coffee yet." She sipped and waited.

"Sleepyhead!" teased Bea. "I wondered whether you could take a few hours to convey an old woman across the lake?" Bea wasn't old—somewhere in her fifties—but did have MS, which meant she rarely drove.

"You mean take the ferry?" a more interested-sounding Gerry replied.

"Yeah! I want to visit the fine food store at the monastery. Make a few purchases. You game?"

"Of course. Oh. I have to shop for a few things in Lovering and do a blood test at the clinic. And I have a few chores to do here. Give me about ninety minutes, okay?"

"Okay. See ya."

After Gerry cleaned out the cat boxes (there were seven in the long narrow bathroom tucked under the main staircase), topped them up with fresh litter, and swept the surrounding floor, she dashed upstairs for a shower. "Definitely a blue jeans and T-shirt day," she muttered into her closet. "Except it may be cool out on the lake." She added a jean jacket, nice soft green paisley scarf and pale blue beret, and turned in front of the mirror. "Looking good, kid!" she congratulated herself before shouting, "'Bye, cats!" and getting into her car.

"Ginger, lemons, sugar," she chanted, entering Lovering's one grocery store. "Sugar, sugar. How much?" She selected the largest bag. "And two lemons." She added them to her basket. As she didn't even know what ginger root looked like and was in a hurry, she asked a depressed-looking boy who was stacking apples. When he directed her to the small pile of twisted golden brown roots, she was dubious. A bit rude, she thought, some of the shapes. She chose a large piece shaped like a person and rushed to the cash.

"So, I told her, I said, 'Don't you be snarky with me, Miss, not after I've cooked your supper *and* washed your dirty clothes.'" The cashier was oblivious to Gerry's hello. She was too busy recounting the previous night's familial misadventures to the next cashier over, who was leaning on the counter.

That lady replied, "Oh, I know. They just don't get it, do they?"

Gerry's cashier announced Gerry's total. Gerry fumbled in her purse. "And then I said, 'Just you wait until *you* have children, Miss. Then you'll see.'" She held out her hand for Gerry's money.

"Oh, I know," her friend repeated. "They're awful." They both looked resentfully at Gerry.

Taking her purchases and change, Gerry slunk out of the store, feeling about fifteen. Then she straightened. Glad I'm not them, she thought, and, leaving the car in the parking lot, dashed across the street to the clinic.

The blood test took no time and soon she was driving the short distance to Bea's house. Her husband Cecil, Cece for short, was hovering around the doorway. He greeted Gerry with a kiss.

A tall thin man with dark hair, he was also Gerry's lawyer. As he worked out of his home, it was only natural he should be there to assist his wife into Gerry's car.

Gerry was glad to see Bea walking with a cane. She could probably have coped with a wheelchair, but it would have been more complicated.

"Having a good day?" she remarked to her friend as they drove away, Bea wiggling her fingers affectionately at her husband.

Bea replied in a quiet voice, "Every day's a good day, Gerry, as long as we're above ground." And pondering that thought, they drove to the ferry, grateful to be alive on such a fine spring morning.

As they passed Gerry's house she said, "You know, Bea, you and Cece are just about the only friends of mine left in Lovering. Doug's camping. Blaise is on that cruise. Andrew is in Arizona helping Markie pack her stuff to move here. And Cathy's so busy in the summer, she doesn't have any spare time."

Cathy Stribling ran a B & B just along the road from Gerry's house. Andrew, Gerry's cousin, lived across the street. He and his partner Markie Stribling, Cathy's older sister, were about to set up house together there. And Blaise, who was in his nineties and who was Gerry's neighbour on the *other* side, lived with his two cats.

"Summer must be when she makes most of her money. And fall, I guess. When does Blaise get back? Where are his cats?" And so, chatting about their friends, they arrived at the ferry landing.

Taking the ferry across the river had to be among Gerry's top Lovering activities, right up there with snowshoeing or cross-country skiing, or just walking in the other three seasons in any of Lovering's woods; and spending time on her own back porch or in the pool during the summer.

Of course Lovering had its share of cultural events—there was a film club, a playhouse, musical performances both home grown and imported, a historical society and two artists' societies—but for Gerry, coming from Toronto where she'd grown up taking the arts for granted, the one thing Lovering had, which Toronto didn't, was its quiet country location. And the ferry provided one of the best ways to take that countryside in.

As it was late on a Wednesday morning, there were only a few cars ahead of them, waiting for the next ferry to arrive. Both women rolled down their windows and inhaled the fresh air. The ferry arrived and was expertly docked by the tugboat operator, who knew just when to cut the engine and pull out of the way, letting the barge coast to shore, the way tugboat operators had been doing at this spot for a hundred years. The sound of planks hitting the deck boomed. Gerry carefully drove her little red and white Mini down then up and parked. Happily, they were at the front of the barge with an unimpeded view.

As the tug roared into life and pulled away, the barge swung in behind it. A man took their money. Bea quipped, "He should charge you half price, Gerry, the Mini is so small."

"Shall we get out?" Gerry asked. When Bea shook her head, she asked, "Do you mind if I do?"

"Of course not. Go ahead. The view is terrific, even from here."

Gerry wrapped her scarf more tightly around her throat and pulled her beret firmly down over her ears. She leaned against the ferry railing and looked upriver.

Fairly wide at this point (the trip would take ten minutes) and, she knew, very deep, the Ottawa River descended from the northwest. She located her land by the small promontory of large rocks that roughly marked where hers ended and Edwina's began. The trees were too thick to see The Maples, but Edwina's large white house next door was visible.

Gerry cursed. She'd meant to bring binoculars on the ride, specifically so she could look at her house. She frowned. Two figures, male and female, had appeared behind Edwina's house. Could the two figures be Edwina and Roald? As she watched, one of the figures, the larger one, the man, threw his arms up in what looked like anger, or exasperation. He got into a bright yellow car parked behind a red one and drove away. The female stood staring after him for a moment, then went into the house.

So that *had* been Edwina. Who else would be entering her house through the back door like that? And probably the man was Roald. But they don't have a yellow car, she remembered, or a red one. I wonder what's going on.

A change in the timbre of the tugboat's engine alerted her that they must be nearing shore. She got back into the car and looked at the approaching village, dominated by a large church almost at the water's edge. A few people were passing the time on the pier watching the ferry dock and its passengers disembark.

The gourmet food shop was less than ten minutes away. During the drive, Bea reminisced about visiting the monastery with her family when she was a child. "So this was the fifties, remember. We'd all pile in the back of the big blue Oldsmobile my dad had—my two sisters and two brothers—and there were no seatbelts, right? So we'd all roll around back there, especially on sharp turns—" Here she put her hand on the dash momentarily as Gerry took one at speed. Then she said calmly, "Like that one. And my brothers would stick their heads out the windows like dogs, you know? Hang their tongues out. And Mum would yell at them."

"It sounds wonderful," said singleton Gerry.

Bea continued, "Sometimes we'd come over to pick apples. You should do that this fall. Sometimes we went to swim at the beach. Then the Ottawa got too polluted and that stopped. But we could still camp there, go for hikes, have picnics. The shop's coming soon. On the right.

"Anyway, I remember one time long before there was a shop or a cheese factory, like there are now, when the monks still made the cheese by hand. Dad had to park outside these big metal gates and leave Mum and us girls in the car. Only men and boys were allowed inside the monastery. My brothers would stick their tongues out at us as they followed Dad inside. Oh, here it is. See if the handicapped spot is free."

It was and Gerry swung into it right next to a ramp. Bea took a handicapped-parking permit out of her purse and propped it in the window. "Prepare to be amazed," she warned, as Gerry helped her up the ramp and into the shop.

It was a wonderful store. They took their time examining the products, most of them artisanal and local or imported from France. Gerry drooled over the cheeses and cured and fresh meats, then was stunned by the number of breads and pastries in the bakery section.

"How will I ever choose?" she wailed. Bea was already filling their cart with her and Cece's favourites. She grinned at Gerry but said nothing.

Gerry decided to buy only things she couldn't purchase on her side of the river. The famous cheese of course, and some local paté studded with whole green peppercorns. A jar of brandied cherries from France. Those would be divine on vanilla ice cream.

The breads had her stumped. Living alone, she rarely got through a loaf before it staled. She selected one wonderful-looking cheese and olive loaf, the cheese oozing out and crusted, the olives large and black; and half a dozen assorted rolls to be frozen and enjoyed in the future.

But the pastry section really brought her to a halt. She felt she was looking at the showroom of a jewellery store; everything was so perfect and shining with glazed fruit or melted chocolate.

Gerry and Bea, who, it must be confessed, shared a love of sweets, stood awestruck, like worshippers before a culinary altar.

"I don't know what to pick. It's too much," breathed Gerry.

As Bea pointed out past winners, Gerry made her selection—all individual portion-sized confections. A chocolate-covered cheesecake which promised a salted caramel-flavoured interior; a cake topped with white chocolate mousse and raspberries; a miniature key lime pie; and a marzipan cat, tinted with orange stripes and sporting a white-tipped tail.

"I'm having a tea party tomorrow and Prudence and I will be baking for that, so I don't want to buy *too* much. The marzipan will keep, won't it?"

Bea nodded. "I don't know about you, but I'm getting hungry for my lunch. Fries and a burger at the ferry restaurant do ya? My treat."

Two happily well-fed women enjoyed the return trip across the lake. When Gerry looked across to Edwina's property, there was no one in sight.

4

Their Churnes and Presses neat, there was no clutt'ry In Pantry, Milk-house, Dairy, nor in Butt'ry. (1654)

Knowing her Aunt Mary was coming the next day, Gerry spent the rest of Wednesday tweaking the house. She and Prudence would give it a good cleaning on the day, but in the meantime, she could tidy. After all, The Maples was where Mary had grown up. She didn't want her aunt to think Gerry was neglecting the house, or getting into slovenly ways.

Prudence would vacuum tomorrow, but would also be baking, so Gerry did what she could. She dusted all the downstairs rooms and decided how and where they'd have their tea: at the table in the living room next to the kitchen. The formal dining room table with its capacity for seating twelve would be a bit much for the four of them, even if one was Prudence's favourite author and the other Gerry's most demanding aunt.

The cats roamed around, unsettled by her busyness. They were used to her more sedentary artistic occupations. She prayed for the next day to be fine so they'd hopefully take themselves out of doors. Aunt Mary wasn't fond of cats, and neither, perhaps, was Edwina Murray.

By five she was ready for a coffee and took it, the slice of chocolate-covered cheesecake and her book out onto the enclosed back porch. Only cats who behaved themselves were allowed out there. No stretching up and hooking onto the floor-to-ceiling screens was permitted. Lightning and Seymour were two who were docile enough, and followed her sedately. Seymour jumped onto her lap while Lightning hunkered down near her feet.

Gerry reached down to fondle the tortoiseshell's ears. Their relationship had come a long way in the last year: from Lightning crouching in a corner of whatever room she was in, tail stump quivering, daring Gerry to approach, to Gerry being able to gently stroke the traumatized beast's head.

Today, for the first time, and to her astonishment, she heard the beginning of a rumble, quickly ended, as if the part of Lightning's body that was involved in purr production was rusty. "Oh, good girl, Lightning," Gerry crooned. The vet had said that maybe the cat's vocal chords had been damaged when she'd been almost burned to death. Smoke inhalation. Perhaps they were regenerating, finally healing. She was still a young cat.

Seymour's purr was quiet but steady. Gerry straightened up and turned her attention to him. "You must give her confidence," she told him. Seymour, his face up-turned, chin resting on Gerry's belly, blinked his one eye slowly, lovingly.

After a late supper of frozen lasagne, bagged premixed salad and red wine (which didn't taste good to her and which she left most of in the glass), and (after much hesitation in choosing) the key lime pie (which tasted just fine) for dessert, when she was tending to the cat boxes in the downstairs bathroom she was struck by a sudden thought.

She stared at the wall behind the toilet, then went out into the main entranceway, turned and looked at the wall behind the wide staircase, beyond which was tucked the bathroom. "I wonder."

She fetched a tape measure and measured the length of the bathroom. Then she walked to the point in the entranceway that was in line with the bathroom door and measured the same distance across the entranceway. The distance covered was barely halfway across the width of the stairs. She got excited and measured the rest of the width of the entranceway, to the wall that separated it from the dining room. "Ten extra feet!" she exclaimed. She ran into the dining room, to the right-hand back corner that should abut the bathroom beyond.

"But it doesn't!" she told the various cats, some of whom were preparing to bed down for the night on some of the dozen towel-covered dining room chairs. She tapped the wall. Hollow.

The corner featured a shallow alcove about one foot in depth, in which were two shelves, the whole finished off at the top with a bit of arched moulding.

Why would the space behind the alcove have been wasted? It could have been a cupboard. Or part of a bigger bathroom. The house's hot water tank was hidden elsewhere in a cupboard and, anyway, it wouldn't have been walled away where it couldn't be serviced. "What could it be?" she asked Bob, who was patiently waiting for her to stop all this random pacing and muttering and come to bed.

She ran back to the bathroom and measured its width, then, dragging the open tape behind her, ran back to the alcove and held it up to the alcove's width. "Exactly eight feet!" she said triumphantly. Bob sat and stared up at her. She dangled the tape in front of him, then released the finger holding it open. The tape disappeared into its case with a satisfying "snick." Bob's eyes widened, so she repeated the trick. He reached up and rested his paws on her leg. She picked him up. "I'm teasing you, aren't I?" she said, nuzzling the soft fur between his ears. She waited for a sneeze but it didn't happen. Good, she thought, so not allergic to cats, hopefully. "I'm sorry, Bob. Let's go to sleep." He jumped out of her arms and preceded her upstairs.

Their other three bedmates—Jay, Seymour and Lightning— were already fast asleep.

She entered an Egyptian tomb and found a rag-wrapped mummy in a stone sarcophagus. There was a wrapped cat mummy at the human's feet. She was just bending over them when—"Dring! Dring!"—the sound of a bicycle bell woke her. She sat upright. "Prudence! Early! Jam!" Startled cats darted away except for Jay, who, perhaps because she was still growing, remained curled on Gerry's pillow, lost to the world, little paws covering her eyes. Gerry threw on her robe and ran downstairs.

Prudence, who was one of the few people who had a key to The Maples, had already let herself in. She unpacked her lunch as Gerry measured coffee into the pot.

"Prudence! You'll never guess what! I found a space under the big stairs, behind the toilet! It's been blocked off by that alcove next to the fireplace in the dining room!"

Prudence lifted one of the boxes of clean Mason jars onto the counter, counted silently, then nodded. "Did you get the ingredients for the rhubarb jam I asked for?"

"Yes, yes," Gerry replied impatiently. "But what about the blocked-off space, Prudence?"

Prudence turned and leaned against the counter. "This house was at one time a store and a post office. The space behind the alcove used to include the space that's now the downstairs bathroom. The store was entered by the shopkeeper from that side and the counter where people were served was where the alcove is now in the dining room. Have you never wondered why there's a sealed door to the outside in the dining room right near the alcove?" Gerry shook her head. "Shall I make the coffee?"

Gerry, who'd not noticed the boiling kettle, moved forward. "No, no," she said. "I'll do it. A store, you say? Do you know when?"

"Not exactly," Prudence replied. "Nineteenth, late nineteenth, early twentieth century, I guess. Maybe Mary will know."

"Hmm. I'll ask her. But why block it off, I wonder? Do you think it would be fun to open it up?" Prudence seemed distracted, so Gerry let it go. "So," she asked brightly, "what's our agenda?"

"You invited Mary for 2:30, so we should be ready for two. First we make the jam and I make the cake. You can prep the scones." Gerry knew what that meant: combine dry ingredients and wet in two separate bowls, ready for the last-minute mixing and gentle kneading that would produce tender fresh scones. "So drink your coffee, go change and we'll pick rhubarb."

Twenty minutes later Gerry met Prudence in the garden, where Prudence was standing ominously over the rhubarb holding a large bread knife. "No! No!" squeaked Gerry. "Please don't cut us, Prudence! Help, Gerry! Help!"

"Shush," Prudence admonished, handing Gerry the knife and bending over the clump. "What if Edwina Murray is out with her dog and hears you?" A sheepish Gerry grinned.

Expertly, Prudence twisted a large outer stalk of rhubarb and pulled. She repeated the motion a further five or six times. Then she took the knife and trimmed the shaggy rough edges from each base and lopped off the giant leaf at the other end. She held the stalks in her hand. "That's about three pounds. You do the same amount again. If we have a bit left over that's fine."

It was Gerry's turn to twist and pull. When she'd finished the rhubarb plant looked only slightly smaller. "Now I see what you mean about keeping on top of the rhubarb, Prudence. We've hardly made a dent!"

"We'll make a couple of pies next week and cut some up into chunks for the freezer."

They walked back to the house where Prudence set Gerry to chopping rhubarb while she prepared the lemons and ginger root.

Gerry retrieved Aunt Maggie's old Lyssex scale from one of the top cupboards. Though its cream paint was scratched and rusty, its green numerals clearly marked a twenty-two-pound capacity. "How old do you think this thing is?" she asked.

"Sixty, seventy years. I have one at home that was my mother's."

"'Patent Swiss Made'," Gerry read, "and 'NOT LEGAL FOR TRADE'. Huh. As in, don't use this for your store. Back to the store, Prudence." Prudence grunted.

Gerry weighed five pounds each of rhubarb and sugar, then dumped them into her largest pot and brought it slowly to the boil. Grated lemon peel, juice and the peeled chopped ginger root were added. "That's it," Prudence said. She put a few little china plates into the freezer of Gerry's fridge. "You'll see what those are for soon," she answered the unspoken question of Gerry's raised eyebrows. "Now you prep those scones while I make my cake."

More lemons were grated and juiced and Gerry understood Prudence was going to make her famous lemon Bundt cake. "Normally, in rhubarb season, I'd make a rhubarb coffee cake—to use up the rhubarb," Prudence explained as she worked. "But as we're serving scones with rhubarb jam I thought a cake full of the stuff might be overkill."

"You seem to be harbouring violent feelings towards the rhubarb, Prudence," Gerry commented as she cut butter into her dry ingredients with a wire pastry blender.

Her friend cracked a thin-lipped smile. "You'll see. Next it'll be gooseberries you have too much of."

"Can we freeze those too?" Prudence nodded and Gerry thought with satisfaction of the small freezer, tucked at the end of her tiny kitchen, soon to be stuffed with summer fruit for autumn and winter baking.

"But they make good jam and chutney too, so we'll make some of that, if you want."

"I'd love to. Then I'll have a pantry full of homemade things in jars like you do. Christmas presents." She covered her dry ingredients, put the wet ones in the fridge and watched Prudence finish her cake and pop it into the oven. The jam bubbled away in its pot, spitting bits of hot syrup on the surrounding surfaces. Prudence took one of the little saucers out of the freezer and handed it to Gerry. "Drip a tiny bit of jam on the cold saucer, tip it so it's a thin puddle, and push at it with a finger." Gerry followed Prudence's instructions then offered her the plate. "Did it wrinkle?"

"Er, I don't think so."

"Wash the saucer, put it back in the freezer and try again with the other cold saucer." Gerry did as she was told but not before furtively licking the sweet'n'sour rhubarb syrup off the plate.

"I saw that," Prudence said with mock sternness. Gerry tested the jam again. No wrinkles. She looked at Prudence questioningly. "Retry every three to five minutes until it wrinkles. Meanwhile you should put the old kettle on to boil."

Gerry hauled out the grey dented kettle that was way too big for day-to-day use. "This thing must be a hundred years old."

"Maybe. Okay, now put the plug in the drain and stand about six jars with their lids in it. When the kettle boils, slowly pour the water over and into the jars and onto the lids. We're sterilizing them." The jam spluttered, the kettle boiled and Gerry followed instructions. Meanwhile, Prudence had tested the jam again. "Here. Look." She prodded the little puddle on the plate with her forefinger. "Wrinkles. It's done."

"Cool!" Gerry said. Prudence put the steaming cauldron of jam on the counter. "Do we put it in the jars now?"

"Wait a few minutes. If you stir it as it's cooling, it prevents the chunks of rhubarb from settling into the bottom of the jars."

"See?" Gerry said admiringly, "This is the stuff they don't tell you in the recipe books."

By the time Gerry had emptied the hot jars of water, almost burning her fingertips, and lined them up on the counter with their lids, Prudence was ready. "Some people use a funnel; I prefer this way." She ladled jam into a large glass measuring cup and poured it carefully into a jar. "Now you take a fresh wet dishrag and wipe the top of the jar. You can put the lids on after that."

The job was quickly done. They stood and admired the six jars cooling on a wire rack. One of the lids made a loud pop. "That means it's sealed," Prudence explained.

"All that rhubarb and sugar for six jars of jam!" Gerry exclaimed.

Prudence scraped the last bit of jam from the pot into a ribbed rolled glass sugar bowl with matching glass top. "That's for our scones later." She put it into the fridge and untied her apron. "Okay. I'm going to vacuum now."

"And then it'll be time for lunch," Gerry said happily. "Do you trust me to take the cake out of the oven?"

Prudence smiled again and said, "I do."

Gerry thought she would give the front garden some attention. There wasn't much of it. But that's what her guests would see first. She fetched her gardening gloves and a trowel from the little potting shed tacked onto the front of the woodshed-cum-garage.

Giant maples, planted close to the road, soared far above her head. A bed of shrubs and perennials to the left of the front door would have looked bare if Doug hadn't planted some interesting pink and pale green striped tulips and ivory daffodils in the gaps there last fall. To the right of the door were more shrubs and a ground cover of periwinkle, a spreading plant whose simple sky-blue flowers would soon fade, but which today were putting on a good show. Gerry spotted some errant grass sprouting there and dug it out. In a few days she would fill the six now empty wooden half-barrels, ranged either side of the entranceway and at the sides of the parking pad, with the red geraniums Prudence assured her were Aunt Maggie's traditional favourites.

She heard the sound of the vacuum cleaner through an open window. A few cars passed by on the road. A bee hummed near the open tulips. "You're early," she told it. "You must be hungry."

Over at the edge of the parking pad, near the potting shed, she saw Lightning and Seymour sitting staring at something near the road. She walked over. "What is it, guys? A bug? A bird?" The two little faces looked gravely up at her. She bent over and patted each one. "You see stuff I miss, eh?" She imagined the cats thinking, "You don't even know how much." From her pocket came the sound of the kitchen timer she'd placed there. "Oops! Gotta check Prue's cake. 'Bye." She entered the house by the nearby kitchen door. The cats' eyes followed her, then their necks swivelled and they assumed their previous position. A breeze blew off the lake and their eyes shifted back and forth, back and forth.

5

The coffee-cups began to clutter. (1808)

Gerry slid the long wooden skewer out of the golden pound cake and tested it for gumminess. It was perfectly dry. "Cake *done*," she said as she removed it from the oven to a rack on the counter. She checked the time. 1:00. Lunchtime.

Prudence joined her and they ate hungrily. Gerry showered and changed. Prudence continued cleaning. At 2:00 they met in the kitchen. "Want to make the scones now while I set the table?" Prudence asked. Gerry nodded.

The scones were quickly assembled and popped into the oven. Gerry had made a simple recipe, substituting buttermilk for regular milk. It gave a nice tang. She went to look at the table Prudence had laid.

A long yellow cloth, gay with sunflowers, their stems providing green accents, had been smoothed over the rectangular table that Prudence had pulled away from the house's lakeside wall. She had arranged four chairs, one on each side of the table.

Each place had a cake plate, a fork, teaspoon and small knife, a teacup and saucer, a glass, and a periwinkle blue cloth napkin. In the centre of the table was a round glass vase with some of the periwinkle plants from the garden cut long so they trailed over the tablecloth.

"That looks lovely, Prudence," Gerry was beginning, when they heard the sound of a car pulling into the circular front driveway. Gerry plucked Jay from the table, where the kitten had been gnawing the periwinkle, and dropped her on the floor. The women each took a deep breath. "Here goes," said Gerry, and walked to the front door.

Aunt Mary stood there with a pot of blue primroses in one hand, her purse and small box of chocolates in the other. "For you," she muttered, holding the gifts out.

Gerry felt tears come into her eyes. "Thank you, Auntie," she managed, and kissed her aunt on the cheek.

Prudence had come into the entranceway.

"Prudence," Aunt Mary said politely and nodded.

Prudence nodded back. "Mary. Let me take your coat."

Mary had dispensed with the sling but one could see as she eased her arm out of her light coat that she was not comfortable.

"Does it still hurt?" Prudence asked, hanging the coat from a hook.

"A bit. It's more stiff than anything." Mary took a tentative step into the entrance hall. "The last time I was here—" She paused.

The last time she'd been at The Maples had been more than six months previously, on the night of Gerry's art party. They all travelled back to that evening when Mary's husband Geoff, though not present at the party, had been alive, and her daughter Margaret, still in her right mind (or so they had thought), had accompanied her.

Gerry broke the painful silence. "Let's go sit down." They went through the formal dining room and then the long hallway where sideboards displayed plates and bowls, glasses and cups, into the everyday dining and living room where they were to have their tea. A few curious cats followed.

"Oh. You put a sofa in here. Good idea." Mary sat on the long dark brown leather sofa with a sigh. Gerry put the primrose and chocolates on the coffee table and sat next to her aunt.

"I'll just put the kettle on," Prudence muttered. The cats ranged themselves around the room. They're probably feeling the tension, Gerry thought.

"The bulbs look nice at the front," Mary said.

"Yes. I'm enjoying them. Aunt Mary, I hope you don't mind. I invited my new neighbour, Edwina Murray, to tea as well." She looked up at the mantel, where the little round brass clock that had belonged to her mother quietly ticked. "She'll be here in a few minutes."

Mary looked interested. "The mystery author?"

"My favourite," said Prudence, sitting down in one of the rocking chairs.

"Oh? And are you joining us for tea?" A trace of Mary's innate insolence towards people who she considered to be servants was just slightly audible.

Gerry took the bull by the horns. "Aunt Mary, you know Prudence has become my friend, as she was Maggie's."

Mary and Prudence looked warily at each other. Mary said, "Well, my sister was always different." Then she looked away, adding, "And lucky."

Gerry supposed Mary was acknowledging that Maggie had been almost universally loved while Mary herself—well, she thought, we'll help her change. She breathed a sigh of relief as the other two women seemed to relax—a bit.

Just then a knock at the nearby kitchen door made them all jump.

"Do you think—?" Gerry began.

"Probably," Prudence finished and got up to see if it was their other guest.

It was.

Edwina Murray entered from the kitchen, Prudence following behind. The author looked flustered, her eyes blinking behind her glasses' lenses. She appeared to be panting. "I'm sorry if I'm late. I was writing. How do you do?" She shook Mary's hand.

Gerry performed the introductions, then she and Prudence served the tea at the dining table.

The majestic lemon Bundt cake, sprung from its fancy mould and lightly dusted with icing sugar, was praised. As were Gerry's scones, still warm, to be dabbed with clotted cream and fresh rhubarb jam.

Prudence had made cream Earl Grey tea in a large ivy-patterned pot and for a few minutes there were only the sounds of teaspoons in cups, knives and forks on plates.

"You spoil us," Mary said. "May I have another small piece of the cake, Prudence?"

"Of course. And I'll send you home with some. You too, Mrs. Murray, if you'd like."

The author nodded, too busy chewing to speak. They waited politely. "Murray is my family name. Roald's name is Henderson."

Gerry interjected, "Er, while I am unfamiliar with your work, Miss Murray, I believe my friend and perhaps my aunt are not." She shut up then, feeling she'd possibly added one too many negatives to that sentence.

Edwina Murray swallowed the rest of her tea. "Call me Edwina," she suggested. She held her cup towards Gerry. "I'd love some cake to take home. My husband would also enjoy it. If he's at home, that is." She looked around. "What a lovely room—all dark and woody with a view to the lake. Not to my taste but I can see its attractions."

Gerry, who was sitting with her back to the view (after all, she lived there and could see it anytime), agreed. "This is where I mostly take my meals. Except in winter when the windows ice up and the view disappears. Then I eat in front of the fire."

"That's not right," Mary chided her. "You must insulate the house. Now you're—" she didn't add the final word but Gerry and Prudence could make a guess that it had been "rich." So the grapevine has relayed news of the sale of the Borduas, Gerry thought. Oh well. It's not a secret.

She nodded. "You're right, Aunt." She turned to Edwina. "Speaking of views, Edwina, yesterday I took the ferry across the river and while I couldn't make out my house very well—too many trees and shrubs—the back of yours was clearly visible."

"Oh? I was in town yesterday," Edwina said.

Gerry blinked, remembering observing the man, the woman, the two brightly coloured cars at Edwina's, and quickly changed the subject. "Did you insulate the house, Edwina? As part of your renovations? And can you recommend someone?"

Edwina nodded. "But I can't remember the name of the company just now. It's a husband and wife. They rip out, insulate, replaster. Phone me and I'll tell you. Which reminds me—do any of you know a good cleaner?"

There was an awkward pause, then Prudence spoke. "I'm a cleaner, Edwina. I clean for Gerry and a few others. How many hours a week were you thinking?"

"Gerry," Mary said rather loudly. "I wonder if you'd take me for a tour of the garden. I'd love to see the spring flowers."

Unusually tactful, Gerry thought, and guided her aunt out the kitchen door, leaving Prudence and Edwina to their negotiations. She herself was wondering who she'd seen behind Edwina's house the day before.

"I use a maid service myself," Mary mumbled. "No need to befriend the help. But whatever works for you." They went down the steps onto the lawn.

"Would you like some rhubarb?" Gerry asked as they passed the plant.

"Huh. I've got my own monster in the garden at home, thank you very much."

"Perhaps you know," Gerry said as they passed the pool, "when is it safe to fill the swimming pool?"

"That was Geoff's department," Mary said. "To call the pool maintenance guy. Any time now, I should think. When we plant the annuals we should be safe from frost. I'm planting mine this weekend. Is that a *Bergenia*?"

Gerry had forgotten this aunt was as keen a gardener as the other one had been. The plant in question, its rhubarb-like leaves and thick stems supporting clusters of tiny mauve flowers, was hideous. But Mary seemed to think it a fine specimen of its kind.

They walked up and down the rows of the rose and perennial garden. Assorted cats frolicked in the shrubbery and on the lawn. Gerry followed them with her eyes. Cats in gardens. Lots of scope for paintings. "Covered in buds," Mary commented, stopping in front of one rose shrub that exhibited a mass of pale yellow ones. Then so softly Gerry hardly heard her, she said, "Harrison's yellow. Geoff's favourite."

This time, Gerry's eyes stung with tears. She'd loved her Uncle Geoff as much for his endless patience with this, his difficult wife, and his ill daughter, as for his kindness to herself. She wiped her eyes.

"That's nice," Mary said. "That he's mourned. I've never been good at the emotional stuff. Shall we join the others?" She gestured towards Prudence and Edwina, who, having come to some arrangement, were now sitting on the back porch with their teacups. Prudence was talking.

"And that part in *Dangerous to Know*, when she's going to go meet him and the reader is still unsure about him and then it turns out it wasn't the one you thought it was who was dangerous to—"

"Don't stop on my account," Mary airily suggested as she sat on a creaky wicker armchair. "I loved *Dangerous to Know*. Gerry, would you get me another cup of tea? And you need to upgrade this old garden furniture." She looked distastefully at the wicker chairs, footstools and tables, all obviously the worse for wear.

Gerry grinned. Up to her old tricks, trying to boss everyone around. "Tea, yes. Furniture, no. I like having a bit of tat around the house. Something I can put my feet on."

When she returned with fresh tea, Aunt Mary was saying, "And I thought your portrayal of the husband's girlfriend in *Purple Angel* was very realistic."

Edwina, seeming more comfortable with Prudence than Mary, flushed and looked down. "Thank you."

Prudence added, "Yes, the description of the difficulties between husbands and wives in *Home to Roost* was accurate, I thought."

"You're very kind," Edwina mumbled. "I kind of forget my books once they're written and published. The one I'm working on is always the most interesting to me."

"I know," interjected Gerry. "When I was writing *Dibble*, I was lost to the world." She stopped, appalled that she was comparing her little self-published children's book to Edwina Murray's no doubt bestsellers.

"Tell me about it," said Prudence, rolling her eyes. Mary snickered.

Edwina said simply, "What's 'dibble'?"

Gerry jumped up and returned with two copies of *The Cake-Jumping Cats of Dibble*, then tried to give a synopsis while her two guests looked at the book.

"You have a vivid imagination," Edwina commented, flipping the pages slowly. "I wish I did. I tend to write what I know, then embroider it."

"Cute," pronounced Mary, after giving the book a cursory look.

"You can keep those copies," an embarrassed Gerry offered. "If you want."

"That would be very nice," Edwina said. Mary nodded. The author continued, "I'll swap you a copy of one of mine." She smiled for the first time that afternoon. "You can get to know my work while I get to know yours."

Gerry was about to say something self-effacing when a bellow from Edwina's garden startled them all.

"'Dwina!" A man's voice roared. Then the man himself, accompanied by his dog, which frisked and jumped happily alongside, came into view. He walked quickly toward the thicket separating the two houses.

Edwina jumped up, turning red. "Sorry," she muttered and looked around, obviously wondering how to escape the porch.

Gerry opened the screen door for her. "Thank you for the tea," the author muttered in a low voice and skittered out onto the stone path. They saw her call and wave to her husband, who angrily stomped back to their house. Edwina was almost running as she turned the corner of Gerry's house and disappeared from their sight.

The three left looked at each other.

"Well," Prudence said calmly. "I did not like that."

"Good-looking man, though," Mary said. "A bit overweight but good-looking."

It was left to Gerry to state the obvious. "Looks like a bully to me. Oh, I meant to give her a jar of jam."

Prudence stood, stacking teacups and saucers. "And I cake. Yes, well, marriages are a mystery to those outside them," she said briefly.

Mary cackled. "You can say that again, Prudence."

Gerry looked uneasily from one to the other. Prudence's husband had been weak and had treated her badly. Mary had treated her own excellent husband badly.

Prudence looked Mary in the eye and said, "So we're in agreement, then." Mary flushed and, seemingly ashamed, looked away and nodded. Prudence added, "If he makes me uncomfortable, *that* job won't last long."

"How many hours did you agree on, Prue?" Gerry said, so casually and with so much affection in her voice that Mary looked at her sharply.

"I said I'd give her one day. Fridays, I think. She liked that, she said, because sometimes she and her husband entertain on the weekend. I start tomorrow."

Gerry whistled. "Fast work, Prudence!" She smiled. "Maybe I'll see you shaking out mats in the backyard."

Prudence smiled back. "Maybe." Then she changed the subject. "Why don't I clean up these tea things and feed the cats before I go? I'll wrap some cake for you to take home, Mary. And Gerry, didn't you want to ask your aunt about the alcove?" She exited with a tray full of china.

"What alcove?" Mary said.

PART 2

PURPLE ANGEL

'Twas the witching hour. Or at least that's what Lovey called it, breathing into Melancholy's ear. Words he remembered from his previous owner. Not words exactly, as the people spoke them. More—a shivery impression.

Not like his name. Lovey was the word he remembered from when he was small and helpless, his special love-word, given him by his person.

Melancholy had no such word, as she'd had no such person. Born on the street to her young mother, who'd walked away from her mewling batch of kittens when she was about to give birth to the next, Melancholy had watched her littermates die one by one. That she had not died she didn't see as a miracle. Her being just was.

Usually the two slept with the girl in her bed, and with Top Cat and Kitten. But tonight they had both woken hours after the girl had snuggled under the covers. They'd stretched and silently padded out of her room. They'd come halfway down one set of the stairs that descended either side of the landing. There they'd stopped and observed the atmosphere of the high-ceilinged entranceway.

The air was musty with traces of the odours of previous lives: people, cats, mice—even dogs, though it seemed this house had always been more an abode for cats than the larger competitors for human affection.

And though not heard in the ordinary way, the place was also alive with echoes from the past, rustling emanations that called or sighed, moaned or whispered.

Along with all this spectral activity were the usual nighttime creaks of an old wooden house, the smell and scrabbling of the mice that lived in its walls. As well there were the doings of the other cats, most of whom were active for part of the night. Only the very elderly stayed snug in a warm place, waking only to observe the antics of the young.

As Melancholy and Lovey sat, The Brothers Three—grey, tiger-striped—slunk past the foot of the stairs, intent on some mission. As usual, the younger thin white, known as Beau, followed the brothers. He spared a glance up the stairs at the two watchers and they saw his thin black moustache change shape as he wrinkled his nose to catch their scent.

The tortoiseshell and the black cat were certainly less visible than the white. But none of them had trouble seeing each other. Their night vision was so similar to that of the day. The greys and blues were more shadowy, darker tinged. That, as well as the sounds, might be one of the things that made nightlife so interesting.

Melancholy and Lovey hopped down the remaining stairs and entered the largest room of the house, the one with the large raised platform in its centre. They heard the tiny noises of cats sleeping. Both of them knew there was something happening by the alcove in one of the back corners of the room; they just didn't know what. As they waited, Lovey began licking Melancholy's ear. She blinked and let her throat relax. The purr stumbled out. Her throat felt better than it had in a long time.

Lovey paused and turned to face the alcove.

The young woman who often stood motionless at the end of the driveway was opening the wall, but just the top half of the alcove. The two shelves with their objects melted away and the woman turned, stood facing the cats over a counter. Her dress was the same one they always saw her in—mauve with black trim. Behind her was a long darkness. But she was smiling.

Leaning on the outside edge of the woman's counter was a young man. He wore trousers and a jacket all in the same colour, with strips of leather crossed on his chest. He seemed to have strips of cloth wound around his lower legs. He also was smiling.

As the cats watched, the darkness behind the woman grew darker and began exerting a pull on her. She receded, her arms outstretched toward the young man.

At the same time, through a hitherto unsuspected door in the outside wall of the house, came a black cloud with a greenish tinge. It seeped into the room at first, wafting around the ankles of the young man, then grew immense, rising until it enveloped him, pulling him down, down.

The cats heard the cries of many people. Their ears went back, tight to their heads. Their fur rose as their skin tingled.

The black cloud completely swallowed the young man. The young woman disappeared into the dark space behind her. The alcove slowly reappeared with its shelves, their jugs and urns.

The cats relaxed. Melancholy turned and licked the slit where Lovey's left eye had been.

6

The musty and dusty clutter and litter of things gone by. (1864)

"Oh, geeez!" Gerry breathed out slowly. She looked around the large basement room filled with metal shelves, each loaded down with cardboard boxes. At one end of the room were black filing cabinets. At the other end, a narrow table and a few chairs. Natural light filtered through foundation plantings, leaking pale and green through long narrow windows high up near the ceiling.

She got up off the floor where she'd been sitting surrounded by editions of the *Lovering Herald* she'd retrieved from various boxes. She had a few papers in one pile, which she took over to the table. She hardly noticed the harsh fluorescent lighting and stale musty smell.

A young girl came halfway down the basement stairs. "Gerry. You want a coffee? Tea?"

"Oh, Judy, that would be great. A strong cup of tea with milk and sugar, please. Shall I come up?"

"No, no. I'll bring it down. I'm all caught up with my work so Dad says I can come help you."

Gerry returned to examining more closely the papers she'd already extracted. She was looking for any mention of when The Maples had been a store and post office. So far, she'd found little to help her. Aunt Mary had been ignorant of any but the same facts Prudence had told her the day before.

Gerry didn't know why she was looking for this information, just that she was. And she was serious about ripping out the alcove. In fact, she'd phoned Edwina's contractors the previous evening and they were coming to give her an estimate at the end of the day.

She wondered how Prudence was getting on with her first day of cleaning at Edwina's. She hoped the husband wouldn't annoy Prudence. She and Edwina had really seemed to hit it off.

Judy—Judith Parsley—came down the stairs with a cup of tea in each hand and a small box of doughnuts under one arm. She carefully set everything down on the table. "Dad says we can finish the doughnuts if we're hungry."

Dad was Bill Parsley, owner of the *Herald*, Gerry's local paper, and Judy was his only child and only full-time employee. They were allowing Gerry the use of the *Herald*'s stacks, which functioned as the town's unofficial archive.

"I'm always ready for doughnut holes," Gerry said rather predictably as the little box was opened. She took a tiny jelly-filled one.

Judy was by way of becoming a friend. She'd taken both the courses of drawing lessons Gerry had offered in her home—one last fall, the other over the winter and spring—and was quite a good artist. Sensitive, Gerry thought.

"What exactly are you looking for again?"

"Exactly?" She dusted icing sugar off her mouth and took a gulp of tea. "I don't know. I'd love to find something about when and why the house ceased to be a place of business. Did the government close it down? Was there competition? Was it for personal reasons? A photo or photos would be great."

"Around what date?"

"Well, my Aunt Mary was born in 1943 and for as long as she can remember back, there was no store. Just the alcove where the store and post office were and the door for customers sealed off."

"So. Pre–Second World War?"

"I expect so. Maybe that was the catalyst for change." In silence they looked through the newspapers she'd pulled out thus far—all from the 1930s. Gerry took a chocolate cake doughnut hole from the box and pensively bit into it. Judy said, "Shall we try the 1920s?"

Gerry nodded. They put away everything from the 1930s and looked at the boxes for the previous decade. "Quite a smaller collection," Gerry commented.

"I think we'll find much shorter papers compared to what we print now," Judith said, taking down the box marked 1927–29.

This box was quickly disposed of. "Look," Gerry said. "Here's an ad put in the paper in May 1928 by another store not far from The Maples. Just down the road in fact. Goodman & Co. General Supplies and Postal Services. We've got something, Judy! We know The Maples' store was already gone. Let's keep looking!"

They went through the box marked 1924–26 again quite quickly. No mention of a Coneybear-owned store. Gerry leaned back in her chair and stretched her arms to the ceiling. "So, Judy, how come not much work today?"

Judy finished her cup of long-cold tea. "Weeklies like the *Herald* are on weekly schedules. Well, obviously. We put the paper to bed—send it to the printers—Wednesday night. It's delivered on Thursday. Dad always takes Thursday afternoons off. Now it's Friday, he's starting to plan next week's edition."

Gerry got up and walked around the room, swinging her arms. "Gosh, I'm stiff. So how long has your family owned the paper?"

"My Grampa James bought it in the 1950s—1952. We celebrated the fiftieth anniversary two years ago. Mum made a big cake—actually, she made several—and we invited the town to drop in on a Saturday afternoon."

Gerry grinned. "I bet they did, too. Loveringians like their desserts."

Judy nodded. "We ran out of cake by two. But it was a nice day. 1921 to 1923?"

Gerry brought the box to the table. Goodman & Co. was regularly advertising in the paper—about once a month. The *Herald* was only eight pages long and the paper had thinned and yellowed with age.

"I found something!" Judy said excitedly. She pushed the paper from January 1921 across the table. "There." She pointed.

Gerry read, first silently, then aloud. "Albert Coneybear, born 1865, died January 6, 1921. Dear husband of Elizabeth (Parsley) Coneybear. Survived by his sons John and Alfred, and his sister Margaret." She felt tears welling up in her eyes. "My great-grampa." They finished reading the 1921 files in silence.

"Let me take you to lunch," Gerry said impulsively, trying to cheer herself up. "You must be getting bored."

"No, I'm interested," Judy protested. "But hungry too."

"Ask your dad if he wants to share a pizza. I like all toppings except pineapple."

Judy smiled mischievously. "Hawaiian's his favourite. We can ask them to do a third of the pizza that way." She ran upstairs and returned shortly. "All done. I got us pepperoni, mushrooms and extra cheese. Okay?"

"I'm already salivating," Gerry replied. "Let's distract ourselves from our stomachs and tackle the next box. Oh look, 1918 to 1920, just after the war."

They read in silence for a while before Judy said, "This is terrible."

Gerry nodded. The obituary section in the various papers had gone from some issues in previous years having no entries, or only one or two, to every edition containing several names of people who had died from either the Spanish flu or "injuries sustained in the recent conflict," which Gerry supposed must refer to lingering wounds caused by the war. The number of young people who died from the flu was surprising. A memory surfaced in Gerry's mind. "I think something bad happened in my grandfather's family around this time. It's on my family tree. Oh, what is it? Two young ones dying around the same time."

"Well, it didn't happen in 1918," said Judith, putting the oldest paper back in its box. A clumping on the stairs distracted them as Bill Parsley approached with an enormous pizza box and a roll of paper towels. He pulled up a chair. "Let's eat!" For ten minutes they attacked their lunch.

Gerry finally leaned back, stifling a burp. "Burt's makes the best pizza." She reached for her third slice and looked narrowly at Bill.

He'd written a piece about her in the paper about a month earlier. A not-too-flattering piece about how hard it was to be a freelance artist, in which he'd said she would "work for kibble." But she'd forgiven him. The article had really been directed at his daughter who had alarmed him by showing strong artistic tendencies. And there was only one paper in town. Gerry needed the *Herald* for advertising purposes.

Bill asked, "Find anything?"

"Not really," his daughter answered. "But we think we're getting close."

"I had a young relative who died in the First World War," Gerry mused. "Alfred. He's on the plaque of the war dead in St. Anne's Church. And his sister, I think, died the same year. I remember thinking what a horrible year that family must have had. I'll check my family tree when I get home. What about you? Judy tells me you're already planning next week's paper."

"Got to. Turnaround is five, six days. There's a spring fair at St. Pete's tomorrow. I'll send my intrepid girl reporter to fight her way to the baking table and cover that." Here he winked at Judy who smiled. "Get some pix. And maybe some cake, eh Jude? Then some pix of the local art group exhibiting at the community centre. We always run a photo of the painting they raffle off and mention who won it. And there's a concert Sunday afternoon."

Gerry marvelled once again at how many cultural activities there were in Lovering. "It sounds like you don't have a lack of material."

"Quite the opposite," Bill said, wiping his mouth. "But the number of articles we can run depends on how many ads we sell. Speaking of which, sorry, Jude, I need you selling on the phone upstairs." Judy got up reluctantly.

"I'll tell you if I find anything," Gerry assured her. "And thanks for your help." After the Parsleys had gone upstairs, she took money for the pizza out of her purse and left it on the table with a short note, thanking them for their records and assistance. Bill had paid when it had been delivered and she guessed would probably not take money from her face to face.

Nineteen-fifteen to 1917. Most of the First World War. She took down the box gingerly, already feeling the weight of the sorrow that had befallen the world during those years.

In 1917, in May, a powder factory had exploded in a nearby town. Gerry's eyebrows rose. What on earth was a factory making gunpowder doing way out in the country? The explanation, when it dawned on her, made sense. Near a rail line but far away from any concentration of people. There had been fifteen blasts over two hours, which had been heard many miles away. One man at the factory had died.

Another man, an unnamed railway engineer, had been a hero. He'd been waiting with his train for a signal to leave the depot, way out in the country past Lovering and past where the explosions had occurred. He was told there were three train cars loaded with explosives, parked near the scene of the accident. So he disconnected his passenger cars and took his engine to the powder company's siding, attached the dangerous cargo and pulled it to safety.

Gerry read how all this had happened while the blasts had been taking place. "Wow," she breathed. "He did well."

Slowly, she worked her way back, finishing 1917, then 1916. In May 1916 the paper ran a poem by Lieutenant-Colonel John McCrae. Once again Gerry read the bittersweet words of "In Flanders Fields."

Soberly she finished 1916 and began looking through papers from 1915, all the while blinking away tears as the obituaries of local boys and men kept coming. She'd forgotten all about the store.

She came to May 1915. Late May. There. Alfred Coneybear, born 1899, missing, presumed dead, sometime during the battle of Ypres in Belgium. A battle that had lasted, or so the paper said, for about a month, beginning in late April, and during which 6,500 Canadians were killed, wounded or captured. The headlines read 2000 Canadians Dead and Poison Gas Used by Our Enemies.

Sadly, she returned the papers to their box. She could always return. But that was enough for today. Upstairs, she forced herself to smile and wave at Judy, who had the phone clamped to one ear and was scribbling madly.

She stepped out into the sweet spring air. Eighty-nine years ago, she thought. Hell on earth.

7

Their sinne…lies cluttered in their soules. (1633)

Gerry bought a few groceries and drove home, passing St. Anne's and its tiny cemetery where her ancestors, including her mother and father, were buried.

Leaning against the side door of her house was a hardcover book. *Dangerous to Know* by Edwina Murray. With an interested murmur, she took it inside. She picked up the nearest cat, who happened to be Mother, her giant marmalade tabby. Mother set up a vast purring and nestled in Gerry's arms until, spying the kitten Jay passing, she leapt to the ground and pinned the kitten, beginning a thorough inspection. Jay must have passed, because Mother reluctantly (or so it seemed to Gerry) released the kitten who scampered out of the room.

"Absolutely no more kittens, Mother," Gerry admonished, shaking a warning finger. "But thank you for cheering me up." Mother blinked and lowered herself onto the hearthrug, her paws tucked under her in that way that always reminded Gerry of Japanese people warming their hands in the sleeves of their kimonos.

She grabbed her sketchpad and produced a cartoon of Mother in a flowered green kimono with bamboo growing behind her. No. She erased the bamboo and arranged the cat in the sketch on a blue pillow with a vase of bamboo canes beside her. When she was satisfied, she tossed the sketchpad aside, after making a notation "cats of the world" at the top of the page.

She walked through into the formal dining room and stared at the alcove. What would she do with the space if, uncovered, it proved useable?

"A nook," she said to several cats who were seated around the huge table. "A work nook. A reading nook. But it'll be dark as I suppose there aren't any windows. Or I could extend the bathroom and put in a door, so we wouldn't have to go all the way around through the entranceway to use the toilet. Nah. The bathroom's big enough."

She went back into the kitchen and made a coffee, then brought it, some chocolate-covered digestive biscuits, and the file in which she kept family history papers to the sofa.

As soon as she sat down, several candidates for her lap presented themselves. She spread a throw over not just her but some of the sofa as well. This let many more cats than could actually fit on her lap *think* that maybe they were. When Bob, Jay, Seymour and Lightning were all arranged to their satisfaction, Gerry opened the file.

The Coneybear family tree was on top. The family had lived in Lovering since the 1830s, when the original John Coneybear moved there. When he married Sybil Muxworthy in 1854 when she was just seventeen and he was forty-four, he'd already built and was living at The Maples.

Six generations of Coneybears had lived or were living in Lovering, so the tree was extensive. Gerry found her great-grandparents and her grandparents, her father's parents—Matthew and Ellie (neé Catford)—and Matthew's siblings—Mary Anne, John and Alfred. Only John and Matthew had survived the First World War. The other two died in 1915.

Mary Anne and Alfred were aged twenty-two and sixteen years old respectively when they died. Their father Albert died a few years later.

Gerry returned the tree to its file and sipped her coffee. She wondered what Mary Anne had died of.

A van with a ladder on top pulled into the circular driveway at the front of the house. Gerry saw a short plump woman get out of the passenger side door and walk toward the kitchen entrance.

"Sorry, cats." Gerry stood up and the cats, annoyed at the too brief cuddle, stood and waited to see what would happen next.

Gerry walked to the kitchen door. The window was open, so she heard the couple's conversation.

"See? I told you to just pull in next to the Mini. It's not like we'd go in by the front door."

The man replied sweetly, "Well, next time, you drive. You do a much better job when you sit in the driver's seat. You can park it where you want to."

"Is that some kind of rude joke? Park it where I—oh, hello, Miss." She'd changed her tone from querulous to sunny mid-sentence. "I'm Lucie Picotte and this is my husband Terry Drugget." The husband was not tall and very thin. Lucie continued, "You called yesterday?"

"Hello. Yes. I want to insulate the house. But I need your advice as how to do that. It's very old and I don't want to change its look. Inside or outside." She ushered them into the little kitchen and from there into the living room.

"Whew!" said Terry. "All wood—walls *and* ceiling!"

"We need to go upstairs," said Lucie. Away they all tramped, trailing an interested group of cats.

"Are you okay with a lot of cats?" Gerry asked worriedly, knowing that some people didn't care for the creatures.

"Oh, yeah," replied Lucie, peering down at the floorboards in what had been Aunt Maggie's bedroom, which four cats in particular still chose as their special place.

From the bed Blackie, Whitey, Mouse and Runt—the Honour Guard, as Gerry thought of them—blinked sleepily. "Cats are fine with us," added Terry, tapping on one of the outside walls. He exchanged a significant look with his wife. "Hollow." He turned to Gerry. "So basically, your heat is passing out through your walls. And probably your attic. Whatever insulation was in there—and they did insulate their walls with horsehair, old newspapers, sawdust—has slipped or shrunk and compacted. Best thing for an old house like this would be foam. We carefully drill holes, then push the foam in where it expands. Or we can remove the interior or exterior walls, depending, and line them with mineral wool."

"Well," said Gerry, who was ignorant of these complexities, "What do you suggest?"

"To be honest—and this is what we did for Miss Murray—I'd remove the walls and line with the wool. We'll be very careful about keeping the walls intact. Foam can be toxic to animals including people. It's good for new houses whose walls are still open. But in old houses, because you can't see it, you can't be sure that you're getting it in all the nooks and crannies."

"Huh. Nooks. You reminded me. Come this way. If you're finished up here." They all trooped back downstairs to the largest room of the house, the dining room. Gerry led them to the alcove. "I wondered if you could rip this alcove out and we could make a little nook for reading or something."

Lucie whipped out a tape measure. "It's five feet across. The alcove, I mean. Pretty narrow," she added doubtfully.

Terry went into the entranceway, then returned. He motioned to the right. "Might be able to extend—with a slanting ceiling of course—under the staircase. Depends what we find behind there." He tapped the alcove wall with his knuckles. "Want us to do this first?" His eyes twinkled. "I'm guessing you're kind of curious."

Gerry smiled. "I *am*. Yes. Do this first. Will you give me an estimate for the whole house?"

Lucie nodded. "Just let us go around again without you. We'll measure exactly how much space there is."

Feeling reassured, Gerry went back to the sofa. It felt good to be finally getting on with the project.

After the renovators left and she had fed the cats, she remembered Prudence, working next door. But it was after five; she must be home already. She decided it would be rude, not only to Prudence but also to Edwina, to appear too curious. If there were anything pertinent to tell, Prudence would share it. But to Gerry, Monday, when next she could expect Prudence, seemed a long way away.

She wasn't yet hungry for her supper—too many cookies with her coffee!—so decided to take the canoe for a paddle. She slipped on her life jacket and a pair of water shoes and walked down to the stony beach. She carefully floated the canoe in a few inches of water. Bob and Jay, who'd followed her to the water's edge, indicated they'd like to join her by to-ing and fro-ing from rock to rock uttering little mews.

She decided Bob she could trust, both to not jump out of the canoe, and to be able to swim to shore if he fell in. She lifted him onto the seat in front of her. "I'm sorry, Jay. When you're a little older." The kitten sat on a rock and watched gravely as Captain Bob with his Able Seaman Gerry floated away.

Gerry paddled east, downriver, passing the wide lawn below the Parsley Inn, where guests ate and drank under red umbrellas on the restaurant's riverside patio. Friday night and the parking lot was full. She wondered if Gregory, one of Jay's littermates, was working inside with his owner Phil Parsley, and pictured the cat parading along the bar.

She guided the canoe between shore and the islet where the Parsleys had set up an old Christmas tree, lit with coloured lights in winter, now just a bare dead thing.

She approached the ferry landing and back paddled, watching a ferry dock, load and leave.

She turned and retraced her way. As she passed the Parsley Inn she thought of Doug who'd used to have a room there, and of how nice it would be if he were in the canoe with her.

"Not that you don't make a great substitute, Bob," she complimented the cat, who turned his head briefly before staring ahead into the dimming light.

Gerry passed her own house—Jay had retreated elsewhere—and decided to paddle a bit longer. She passed Edwina's and sure enough, as Edwina had explained to Prudence, the couple appeared to be entertaining. There must have been six or eight cars pulled up in the wide dirt and gravel driveway that girdled the back of the long low white house. Gerry looked for the yellow car she'd seen from the ferry. It was not in evidence. But the red car was.

Lots of people have red cars, she told herself. And, that a circular driveway is good for parking but she wouldn't want to give up that much of the garden. Though the garden that remained was sizeable, bigger than that at The Maples.

Windows in Edwina and Roald's house were open. Music and laughter trailed out into the night. It's good the house is inhabited again, Gerry thought, thinking of its recent and not so recent sad past. She went a little further but, as dusk advanced, decided to call it a night. She dug in her paddle and held it and the canoe slowly turned.

As they again passed Edwina's house, Gerry heard Roald talking loudly then laughing in the backyard. By a small glowing point in the near-dark she guessed he was enjoying a cigar. The woman at his side was shorter than Edwina and, as he pressed her to his side, she laughed too, looking up at him. He bent his head to kiss her.

Then, as Gerry watched, frozen in surprise, Edwina came out of the back door of the house, saw her husband and the woman and immediately turned around and went back in.

Gerry paddled as quietly as she could towards home. She doubted the couple had heard or seen her, or Edwina, they'd been so caught up in each other.

She heated a can of ravioli and dumped some premixed salad on a plate with a frown wrinkling her brow. Was Roald's girlfriend something she should keep secret, even from Prudence?

She took her supper with a glass of red wine onto the back porch. She listened again to the sounds of the party but now they gave her no pleasure.

She fretted as she tried to sleep, and when she woke up, she'd decided it was none of her business what the state of Edwina's marriage was.

She made herself a nice Saturday morning kind of breakfast— kippers, scrambled eggs, buttered toast and a pot of Irish breakfast tea—then went outside with a little notepad and pen. She would make a list of all the plants she needed to buy.

First: annuals for all the half-barrels at the front of the house. Red geraniums and some trailing ivy-like stuff. Second: vegetables. She remembered what Doug had planted, unbeknownst to her at the time she'd been settling in to her new abode the previous spring. Tomatoes and green peppers. Okay, those came already started. She knew that much! Then the things that came from seeds. Peas, beans, carrots. She smiled. This would be fun. She set off for the nursery.

At least half of Lovering must have had the same idea. The nursery's parking lot was full, so Gerry found a spot with many others parked along the highway. She walked to the little shop in front of the greenhouses. Seeds first. She hummed and hawed over all the varieties. Edible podded peas seemed thrifty and she wouldn't have to shell them. She took scarlet runner beans for their red flowers. Carrots and purple bush beans should be enough.

She waited until a customer was finished unloading purchases into their car, then took their trolley. Now for the plants.

Gerry loved cherry tomatoes so took a few plants of those: yellow pear, red pear and the usual globes. She also loved the big fleshy juicy tomatoes, perfect for toasted sandwiches with cheese, lettuce, black pepper and salt, and plenty of mayo. She selected four plants. Did she really need green peppers? She didn't cook much and didn't enjoy them raw. Instead she decided to try a couple of hot red pepper plants. The little fruits looked so cute on the picture in front of the row of plants.

She spent a lot of time dithering in the herb department. Dill, coriander, parsley and thyme were her final selections. Then she went back and bought four basil and four catnip plants. She wanted to make her own pesto and had a plan for the catnip. Her little car was packed.

When she got home and the plants were all lined up next to her shed she was appalled. So many! What had she done? But they did look nice, massed against the wood side of the shed. She wandered down onto the lawn and cautiously looked towards Edwina's house. All was quiet.

Must be sleeping in after their big bash, she thought virtuously. It was eleven o'clock and *she'd* already been out and back. As she watched, a car pulled into Edwina's driveway and two men got out. They knocked at the back door and were admitted. Aha, thought Gerry, someone's up.

She went inside and turned on the valve for the outside water tap. Then she got her garden hose out of the shed and attached it before unwinding it near the garden. She began to dig holes.

After a while she paused for lunch. She had store-bought tomatoes and made the sandwich she'd been fantasizing about at the nursery. She made a diagram showing where vegetables should go. Then she got back to work.

At around three that afternoon she stepped back in relief and surveyed the garden. She'd made the plants her priority, so they were all in. Except for three of the four catnip plants, which were part of an experiment, and which were going into the shed for the time being. She'd plant the seeds the next day, Sunday. It all looked very nice.

The gooseberry and currant shrubs were in flower—their delicate blooms an interesting chartreuse. Alliums had opened their purple globes. Bees hovered over every available source of nectar or pollen. Cats, who had been supervising Gerry, now busied themselves with hidden rustles and chirps that needed their attention. The older ones dozed in the sun.

The apple tree, in flower a few weeks ago, was almost all green now, its new leaves uncurled and fresh looking. She'd repaired the hole made by the excavations of Jay the kitten, also a few weeks earlier.

As she made a few trips putting away her tools and the empty plant pots in the shed, Gerry noticed Lightning and Seymour, again sitting quietly near the road, fixating on a point above their heads. She walked over and sat on her haunches. "What *is* it, guys, that's got your attention? A nest of baby birds?" She didn't hear any peeps.

There was no way the cats could tell her. As she turned to go, a breeze blew off the lake onto her bare arms. And she shivered.

8

An unwieldy and overgrown establishment, cluttered with furniture. (1854)

"Gerry." The quiet voice right behind her made Gerry jump. If one could jump when kneeling. She was sowing carrot seeds and had just gotten to the end of a row, was beginning to backfill the tiny trenches and press the seeds into close contact with the earth.

She turned and saw Edwina Murray standing next to her, twisting her hands together. She must have come noiselessly across the lawn. "Gerry. I don't know what to do." For a change, Edwina didn't look distracted. She gazed down at Gerry with perplexed eyes.

Gerry scrambled to her feet. "What is it, Edwina?" She hoped the author wasn't asking for help with a wayward character or her plot. She didn't feel qualified to advise on literary matters.

"It's Roald." Her voice trembled. "He's missing. I think—I mean, his car's there, but he isn't. It's almost two days now."

"Yes?"

"I think he's gone off with—someone." A tear trickled down Edwina's cheek.

Inwardly cursing—that ended her chance to finish seeding her garden today—Gerry led Edwina to the side of the house.

"Just let me put on the kettle and change my clothes." She dashed upstairs, dropped the pair of old sweatpants, their knees encrusted with soil, on the floor and pulled on a clean pair.

Edwina was still standing in the living room, staring out the window at the lake. Now she was fidgeting with her wedding ring, running it up and down her finger. She turned to Gerry and spoke, her voice hard. "He's done it before, you know." Then she faltered. "Just, not for so long."

"Sit down, Edwina." Gerry indicated the sofa. "I'll make tea and then we can chat." Gerry looked around. "Here," she said, picking up Min Min, her elderly white cat, and plunking him on Edwina's lap. "I know you prefer dogs, but cats can be very comforting when we humans are distressed. And this one's a sweetie." As if to prove her right, Min Min began purring.

Gerry brought a tea tray into the room and put it on the coffee table. She sat next to Edwina and poured her a cup. "Cookie?" She offered the few remaining chocolate covered digestives.

Absentmindedly, Edwina took one. Gerry put a cup of tea in front of her. Equally absentmindedly, Edwina's other hand rhythmically stroked Min Min.

Hah, thought Gerry. When needed, apply one cat. "Thank you for the book. I've already started it." Edwina nodded distractedly. "So, tell me all about Roald. If you want to."

"Oh. Everybody knows Roald plays around," Edwina said matter-of-factly. She added quietly, "I earn the money. He spends it."

Gerry didn't know what to say. Things were moving so quickly. In a couple of days, they'd gone from discussing books to the intimate details of Edwina's marriage. "I'm—sorry?" she said tentatively.

Edwina waved a hand deprecatingly, sending a shower of cookie crumbs into their immediate vicinity. Mother, sitting on the hearthrug, nosed around on the carpet for some of them. "Oh,

I'm used to it. And if it means I don't have to—" She stopped and a slow blush bloomed on her throat and crept up her face.

Gerry guessed her husband's infidelities meant she could forego performing her "wifely duties." Never having been married, she didn't have any experience with this type of thing. She also blushed and cleared her throat. "When did you last see him?"

"Friday night. We had a party." Wryly, she added, "You may have noticed." Gerry nodded. "Roald likes parties and I don't mind. I'm alone with my writing most days. People are interesting to watch. I get ideas for my books." She paused.

Gerry refilled their cups. "Go on."

"Roald's 'friend' these days is a woman called Andrea. She was married, but to a much older man. He died. She had another husband but they divorced. Then she moved on to Roald."

Min Min had stopped purring and gone to sleep. Edwina's hand lay lightly on him. A few other cats had drawn close to the women. Little Jay was fast asleep on Gerry, while Lightning and Seymour had joined Mother on the hearthrug. As usual, Bob supervised everyone from his perch on the mantelpiece.

"How does he get up there?" asked Edwina.

"He's a mighty leaper," Gerry replied. "Er, I think I saw Roald and Andrea Friday outside your house. I was canoeing and… and…you came out and saw them too."

Edwina hung her head in shame. "You must think me a poor creature."

"It's not for me to say," Gerry began.

Edwina burst out with: "He'll take half of everything if we divorce! Half of my earnings. And my savings. For my retirement. I'll have to sell the house and give him half the money." Her voice became passionate. "And I love that house. I waited a long time for it." She stopped, aghast at her own candour, no doubt, and abruptly stood.

Gerry moved fast and managed to half catch, half guide to the rug an astonished Min Min.

Edwina was already in the kitchen. "Thank you for the tea." Then the door slammed.

"Well!" said Gerry to the assembled company. "Her second dramatic exit!" The cats, used to the unpredictability of humans, blinked.

The phone rang. "Doug!" She forgot all about Edwina Murray. "How are you? Where are you calling from?"

"From the campground," he replied. "How are you, love?"

"Oh, I'm great. I've been planting the garden."

"Doing me out of a job?" His voice sounded amused. Not only was he Gerry's boyfriend, he was also the house's handyman-gardener.

"Well, I'm on vacation too, you know, and I've discovered I quite enjoy getting my hands dirty. How are the boys?"

"Good. They're good. We've rented a canoe and two of us are usually out in it at any given moment." His voice softened. "I miss you, you know."

Gerry's heart warmed. As a couple, they'd had their ups and downs, mostly involving Doug's ex-wife (and Gerry's cousin) Margaret. "I miss you too, Doug. When are you coming back?"

"In a week. As planned. I'll see you next Sunday."

"Okay. Another week. Well, I'm getting to know the new neighbours—Edwina and Roald. And—oh, Doug—can I fill the pool now?"

"Yeah. No frost where you are. Frost still in the mornings up here. Cold at night. If only—never mind. Next time we'll go camping together, you and me. The pool. Yeah. Just put the hose in it and leave it on."

"How many hours will it take?"

He laughed. "How many hours? How many days, you mean. Check it after a day and a half. Watch out the water pressure in the house doesn't drop. You might want to turn off the outside water if you're doing a laundry."

"Will it affect flushing the toilet?" Gerry asked in a worried voice. She'd already had country plumbing difficulties, hopefully resolved, almost from the moment she'd moved in to the house.

"You'll find out," he replied in a cheerful voice. "Oh, David's waving. He's finished in the camp shower. My turn. A nice cold shower. Brr. Just what I need. Okay. Love you. Love you."

"Love you." She hung up and turned to the cats. "Right. We might as well start now."

She went outside to set up the hose. When she'd dragged it from the garden to the edge of the pool, she stopped. "But I thought I just cleaned this out," she muttered, looking at the irregularly shaped mass of twigs on the pool's floor. Grumbling, she went to get the ladder and a garbage bag and began throwing bits of the mass up over the pool's edge. Ronald and the three grey tiger-striped cats Winston, Franklin and Joseph—whose special area of the garden this was (known as Yalta, for historical reasons) — peered down at her and chased the bits that appeared up at their level.

Some of the sticks seemed stuck together and she recoiled as she realized most of them were covered in bird poo. "Yuck!" She was glad she had on gloves. As she worked at dismantling the mass, she began to find objects. A piece of an aluminum pie plate, a small sparkly plastic ball, even a fork she recognized as being one of hers. "What on earth?"

A croak from directly overhead drew her attention upward. Two crows sat in the scantily leafed willow that shaded the pool. "Is this your nest?" she asked. The crows looked at her, shifting their feet on the branch. "Did it blow down? I suppose that ring I found belongs to you?"

She mounted the ladder and bagged the debris. She draped the end of the hose over the side of the pool. She put away the ladder and turned on the water. Then she ran back to the pool. The hose had lifted itself out of the pool and was watering the lawn and nearby cats, two of whom were drenched. She stifled a snort of laughter as the cats dignifiedly stalked away. It doesn't do to laugh at cats in their discomfiture, she had learned. She pushed more of the hose down and this time it stayed. "Sorry about your nest," she said to the crows and went into the house.

She quickly ate some lunch, showered and changed. Earlier that morning she'd had an intriguing invitation to tea and she didn't want to be late.

As one of the people she was meeting was a special case, she called ahead to say she was on her way. She listened as the usual whispered conversation between the person who'd answered the phone and the other person took place. As she drove to the heart of Lovering, she wondered how the visit would go.

At the end of one of the village's side streets stood a small grey and white cottage—grey stucco with white wooden trim and a dark grey roof. The yard was neat. There didn't seem to be any gardens.

Gerry parked and got out of her car, holding a jar of rhubarb jam. She rang the front door bell and waited. And waited. Finally, she heard shuffling from inside, and guessed a final whispered conversation was ensuing.

The door was flung open. "Hello!" said the man who stood there. "I'm Gordon." Balding, with glasses, and a big stomach supported on a large frame, Gordon Conway stepped to one side, revealing his wife June, one of Gerry's art students.

June was very short and very fat and stood sideways, looking neither at her husband nor at Gerry. She kept her eyes half-closed and clutched a fluffy grey cat to her chest.

"Hello, Gordon. Nice to meet you. Hello, June. This is for you." As Gerry offered the jam, the cat used June as a springboard and leapt to the floor, then dashed outside.

"Thank you," whispered June, rubbing her arm where the cat had scratched her, and took the jam. Gerry stepped through the doorway and gasped.

To say the house was over-furnished and over-decorated would have been an understatement. Walls were invisible. All manner of shelving went from floor to ceiling in the narrow hallway that extended from the front to the back of the house, making it even narrower.

Yet as she followed June down the hallway, Gerry felt she wasn't walking through someone's home but through a strange art installation.

On the shelves were no mess of random objects, but carefully curated collections. Here were several feet of small plastic trolls with outrageously coloured hair, and their furniture. Below them were ranged tiny models of rocket ships. And below that was a row of ceramic bowls, all by the look of them belonging to probably the same maker.

Above their heads, streamers, strings of coloured beads and Christmas lights twinkled and sparkled. On the top shelves were stacked wrapped and beribboned packages in all sizes. As they passed the banister leading upstairs, Gerry noticed that ceramic horses had been glued to it. The staircase turned halfway up. The banister and its horses likewise turned, cantering upstairs. A bemused Gerry followed June into the kitchen.

The kitchen was just a normal, if a bit cluttered, room. Several sideboards displayed different collections of china, among them the British royalty commemorative mugs, trays and ashtrays June cherished. Gerry spied the mug she'd given June, who continued to speak in a whisper. The only words Gerry could make out were "Tetley," "Bigelow" and "Typhoo."

"Oh, I don't mind," said Gerry. "Any kind of tea will do."

June paused and Gordon laughed. "She's not asking you about tea! She's telling you the names of the cats. The grey one who went outside is Tetley. Bigelow is this handsome guy." He indicated a sleek black cat sitting on a padded rocker. "And this beauty—" He picked up a longhaired calico that looked a lot like Gerry's old cat Marigold, now sadly deceased. "This is Typhoo."

Gerry laughed. "Well, I'm glad to meet everybody." She petted Typhoo. June was busy making tea. Gerry and Gordon sat at the table. And Gerry asked the question everybody asks everybody else when they meet for the first time. "So, Gordon, what do you do?"

"Do? Do?" he boomed. "I'm a train engineer."

"Really?" June brought the tea to the table. "Passenger trains? Freight trains?"

"Well, I started on freight but, boy, that's hard work. Long hours, never know when you'll get home. I did it for a while. Then I thought, better leave that to the younger fellas. So I did. Applied to work the Lovering–Montreal run, and, after a few years, I got it. It helps that I live out here at the end of the line. Oh, those look good, Juney." He gestured for Gerry to select first from a tray of miniature pastries.

Gerry hesitated. She'd been eating a lot of sweets lately, still had lemon cake at home and two of her gourmet shop purchases. But June would be disappointed if she didn't eat. June joined them at the table. "Did you make all these, June?" June nodded. "Wow. What an assortment. I'm going to have a pecan square and an almond tart. To start."

"She bakes almost every day," Gordon said proudly. "She freezes most of it. For another day. I'm a lucky man." One of his large hands gently patted one of June's small plump ones resting on the table. "Tell Gerry what you do with your time when you're not doing housework, Juney."

June bent over and picked up Typhoo and cuddled her. She whispered, "Dioramas."

Gerry wasn't sure she'd heard correctly. "Diagrams?" she repeated, a little puzzled.

"Dioramas," June repeated, marginally louder.

Gerry nodded to show she understood and repeated the word. "Dioramas."

"Maybe she'll show you some later," suggested Gordon. June nodded.

"How old are the cats?" Gerry asked, just to make conversation.

Later, Gordon went to putter outside and June took Gerry into her workshop, a little room off the kitchen. A big table was in the centre. There was barely room for them to edge around it. At one end were the unfinished pieces; at the other, a few finished ones.

Gerry took it all in and marvelled. One tiny scene, barely a foot high, a foot and a half across, was of a train pulling into a station. An engineer, obviously Gordon, hung out of a window and waved and smiled down at a little round June on the platform in front of an old-fashioned train station, like the one in Lovering. Their three cats sat sedately next to her. What made the scene beautiful was the flock of grey pigeons, each one a half an inch in size, which was in the act of lifting off from the platform.

Another diorama pictured a little girl sleeping in a dark wood, a red fox curled protectively around her, other animals nearby. White star-shaped flowers dotted the forest floor.

"June! These are lovely! You are so talented."

June smiled and flushed and brought out other treasures from under the table. A pond where pink origami frogs rested on giant lily pads, while squirrels seemed to run up and down heavy-looking vines. A living Christmas tree in a snowy forest, decorated with shining red hearts, with footprints in the cotton batting snow leading to and from it. The inside of an old-fashioned store. A pretty girl in a mauve dress stood behind the counter. The words POST OFFICE appeared above her head. A young man dressed as a soldier leaned on the counter. By his feet sat two cats: a tortoiseshell and a black shorthair. The tortoiseshell had no tail.

"Oh, that's so sweet—you used two of my cats as models."

June shook her head. "I see them," she whispered.

"The cats?"

June nodded. "Yes. All the scenes. I see them."

Thinking she was describing her artistic process, Gerry nodded. "I see my art in my head before I actually do it too."

June frowned and seemed to think for a moment, then pushed the diorama of the store toward Gerry.

"Really? It's for me?" June nodded. "Thank you very much. I love it. And there used to be a store and post office at my house, so it's very appropriate. I'll display it with pride."

Back in the kitchen, Gerry saw it was four o'clock. Outside, Gordon seemed to be playing ball with Tetley, throwing tiny pompoms for the cat to pounce on. "Well, I should be going. It's almost cat feeding time at my place. Thank you for the tea. And for the diorama." Gordon and Tetley came in from the backyard. "Nice to talk with you, Gordon. Maybe I'll see you on the train sometime." She wiggled her fingers at Tetley, Bigelow and Typhoo. "'Bye, cats."

She carefully put the miniature store on the floor of her car. When she got out at home, she saw there was a large dark car pulled up behind Edwina's house. She hesitated, then went inside, arranged the diorama on the table in her entranceway and went to feed her cats.

Later, after supper, and when she was watering her tubs of geraniums in front of the house, she saw a police car turn into Edwina's driveway.

9

All the clutter will be hushed. (1669)

"You'll never guess what," were the words Gerry chose to greet Prudence when she let herself into the house Monday morning.

"No, *you'll* never guess what," replied her friend, pouring herself a mug of coffee and leaning against the counter. She wore her work "uniform": grey pants and a white shirt with a black sweater. Riding her bike had put roses into her cheeks and loosened her hair, and as she was smiling at a sleepy Gerry, still in her robe and slippers, Gerry thought, for a minute, that Prudence almost looked pretty.

"All right," Gerry yawned. "You go first." They carried their mugs to the living room sofa. Cats, having but recently breakfasted, strolled by, their bellies full, or paused for post-prandial grooming.

"It's a good thing there's nothing wrong with your health," Prudence began mysteriously.

"Why?"

"Because Dr. Barron was cleaning out her gutters on Saturday and fell off her roof."

"No!"

"Yes! She's not in danger but she broke an arm and a leg and has a slight concussion."

"That's awful!"

"I know! And the worst part for Lovering is that she's our only doctor. Now we'll have to go to a clinic or even the hospital when something's wrong with us."

"Well, so far so good," said Gerry, knocking knuckles on the coffee table. Nearby cats paused and waited for the imagined person at the door, then returned to their activities.

"What's your news?" Prudence asked, shifting her legs so Mother could jump onto her lap. Mother kneaded her claws, turned and settled.

"My news? Well, not really news, just—on Sunday morning, when I was planting seeds in the garden—"

Prudence interrupted. "The geranium tubs look very pretty."

"Thank you. So Edwina Murray appeared and wanted to talk about her husband."

"Oh yes," Prudence said grimly.

"Well, she seemed distressed so I brought her in for a cup of tea." Gerry recalled the conversation. "Actually, looking back on it, I think she was more upset at the prospect of divorcing him and losing half her property than the fact that he'd been missing for a day and a half."

"Missing, eh? Hmm. He's a leech," Prudence pronounced.

"That's what she said. But she must have loved him once, because she cried a little too."

"Poor woman, she'd be better off alone." Prudence leaned forward. "I don't want you to think I gossip about my clients with other clients, because I don't, but when I was cleaning her house last week, she was very happily writing away in her study. Then *he* barges in, all loud and angry, and she scuttles past me to get her purse. I swear we all breathed a sigh of relief when he left. Except for the dog. The dog loves him."

"Dogs don't judge," Gerry said softly.

"Like me, you mean?" Prudence said, rather huffily, drawing herself up.

"Like *us*," Gerry reassured. "I don't like him either. Anyway, he's been missing since Friday night. Apparently, it's not unusual for him to go off with—ah—a lady friend. And last night, a police car was at the house."

"Huh. Well, I only clean there on Fridays so I suppose he'll be back by then. Meanwhile—" She rose. "Better tackle this place."

Gerry also rose. "And I shall work in the garden."

The garden was redolent with the scent of honeysuckle and lilac. She inhaled mightily, then went to look at the catnip plant she'd planted two days before. Gone. Eaten down to the ground and then, apparently, dug up and rolled on. "Huh. This is going to be harder than I thought." She went and got a second plant from the shed and planted it in a different place. "Good luck," she wished it, her voice expressing her doubt.

Later, after all her vegetable seeds were in the ground and she'd eaten her lunch, Gerry was taking a break from *Dangerous to Know* and starting to read the third in the Swallows and Amazons series—*Peter Duck*—which purported to tell of pirate treasure and other adventures on the high seas, when she saw a car arrive at Edwina's house. Two men in suits got out of the car and were let into the house. Gerry felt confused by the number of cars and men who were visiting at Edwina's. This pair stayed there for a long time. After the car left, Gerry dithered for a moment, then went to find Prudence, who was giving the bamboo room a good dusting.

It was Gerry's favourite room in the house, though it was unusable for most of the year due to its lack of insulation. Being able to use it again made her feel like she was meeting a long absent friend. She sat on one of the low green banquettes that formed an 'L' in one corner. Prudence stopped taking ornaments off one of the built-in glass-fronted bookcases.

"What?" said Prudence, looking aggravated at being disturbed.

"Another car just came and went from Edwina's. It looked like a cop car, but unmarked. It had that antenna thing they have on one side of the roof. And two guys in suits and topcoats got out and stayed there for about an hour. I don't know. I feel uneasy."

"So go see," suggested the ever-practical Prudence. "Be neighbourly."

Gerry thought for a moment. "All right. I will."

Rather tentatively she walked the short distance to Edwina's house, then hesitated. The other visitors had used the back door.

She walked around to the back of the house. It was very quiet. As she knocked, she heard a squirrel chittering from a nearby tree and from inside the house, a muffled bark.

A pale, bewildered-looking Edwina opened the door. Shadow stood by her side, leaning against her leg. Gerry cleared her throat nervously. "Edwina, I saw the police car last night and that you had more visitors just now and—"

"He's dead," Edwina said bleakly. "Roald's dead." The dog uttered a long slow whine and Gerry saw that the black hair running down his spine was rising.

10

Villainy...clutters together in Heaps, and where you find one, all the rest are not far. (1734)

"And then she just closed the door," Gerry concluded. "She's a very abrupt person."

"That's two," said Prudence, sipping her tea.

"Two what?"

"Two bad things. They come in threes. First Dr. Barron and now Edwina's husband."

"Oh yeah. I forgot—Science." Gerry grinned at her superstitious friend.

Prudence made a face. "You'll see. Oh, I brought you a copy of one of Edwina's books—*Purple Angel*. If you want to borrow it."

"Oh, thanks. Edwina left me another one—*Dangerous to Know*." Gerry showed Prudence the cover of *Dangerous to Know*. A key lay on the ground and a woman stooped to pick it up. In the distance was the back of a man, walking away after having presumably just dropped the key. It was night and a streetlight shone down on the scene. "I've already started it. So who or what is dangerous to know?" Gerry asked.

"I'm not telling you that!" a scandalized Prudence replied. "That would spoil the book for you." She picked up *Peter Duck* and sniffed deprecatingly. "What are you reading this for? Research?"

Gerry replied dreamily. "Not really. They were Dad's. That's one reason. It's nice to hold something he used to hold. And it's just—a childhood I could never have hoped to have. The kids in the book all have siblings. I didn't. They go away to boarding schools, then have wonderful country vacations on their holidays. I lived with my parents in Toronto and our vacations were spent either there or here, visiting family. So—I read them for escapism."

"Oh. Well. I suppose that's why I read Edwina's mysteries." Prudence blushed. "There's usually a romance in them."

"Oh ho! Now we're getting to it! Well, I'll finish *Dangerous to Know* and let you know what I think." She took back her children's book. "But first I have to find out if Roger becomes an able seaman or not."

Prudence rolled her eyes. "What's that thing in the foyer?"

"What thing?"

"The little box with people in it. It looks like a scene from a play."

"Oh, that's one of June Conway's dioramas. They're exquisite. She's got loads more at her house."

"Hmm. I feel I've seen that scene or those people before. Oh, well. It'll come to me." She went to do cat laundry and Gerry relaxed on the back porch. It was an idyllic afternoon. She'd just closed her eyes when the slamming of car doors roused her.

The same car as earlier that day. The same men walking towards Edwina's back door. A pause. Then Edwina, clutching her purse to her chest, was ushered by one of the men into the back of the car and driven away. The other man opened and looked into the trunks of Edwina and Roald's, cars then got behind the wheel of one and drove it away. Gerry wondered if Edwina would have to identify Roald's body and shuddered. Poor woman. She tried to return to her book but it suddenly seemed puerile. She opened *Dangerous to Know*. The phone rang a few minutes later.

The last person she would have expected to hear spoke. "Gerry," said Edwina Murray. "I need your help."

Gerry replied, "Of course, Edwina, what is it?"

"Um, I'm not at home right now. Could you, uh, feed and let Shadow out? Around five o'clock?" She broke off as a muffled male voice spoke. Gerry waited. "Gerry?"

"Yes?"

"I may be detained for some time. Roald was shot. The police have questions." She paused. Gerry digested this information. "Would you be able to look after Shadow until tomorrow? Tomorrow sometime?"

Gerry, who'd looked after her friend Cathy's dog, Prince Charles, for a couple of days when she was in hospital, knew a bit about the ways of dogs. A bit. "Yes. Of course I can, Edwina. Is there a number at which you can be reached?"

"Not really," Edwina replied miserably. "I'm at the police station in—" and here she named a somewhat larger village about a fifteen-minute drive from Lovering, Lovering being too small to merit its own station. "But I hope to be home tomorrow. Thank you."

And Gerry was left staring at the phone, listening to the dial tone. "Prudence!" she shouted.

Prudence, who had been placing clean towels on the upholstered dining room chairs, came running. "What? What?"

Solemnly, Gerry said, "It's the third bad thing."

After agreeing with Gerry that Edwina's predicament certainly looked suspicious, Prudence left for the day and Gerry fed the teeming multitude of hungry cats. The timing was good as it meant that the cats would be busy in their house instead of following her to the dog's house. It was with some doubt that she walked over to Edwina's. There was a key, Edwina had said, hidden high up on a ledge above her back door, so Gerry, being a short person, had come prepared with a folding two-step ladder. She positioned it in the doorway and quickly found the key. Slowly, she opened the door.

Shadow was sitting inside. He looked at Gerry. His face was hard to read. Cathy's basset cross, Charles, moped from room to room of Cathy's large B & B and showed his affection by plunking a drooling muzzle in Gerry's lap; and Harriet the husky (now moved away with her owner Jean-Louis), who would knock Gerry over in her enthusiasm, *and* with whom Gerry had formed a mutual admiration society, were dogs easy to understand. Shadow was not.

Gerry stood in the doorway for a moment, holding the key, then put it in her pants' pocket. The dog was neither wagging his tail nor was he growling. She decided talking to him, the way she would talk to her cats, might be a plan.

"Hello, Shadow. I'm awfully sorry to hear about your master." The dog looked up motionlessly. "And I'm afraid Edwina has to be away for a little while." I hope a little while, Gerry thought. The dog remained impassive. "Supper?" she asked.

The dog stood, stretched, bowed and stalked down a hallway. Gerry, who hadn't been in the house since it had been refurbished, followed. After a few paces, the hallway turned right and opened out into the kitchen, a long room that ran along part of the back of the house. The old cupboards had been replaced with new modern ones below grey countertops, while above were no cupboards at all, but open shelves, where Edwina's plates and glasses sparkled in full view. Gerry liked the effect.

She looked around for the dog's dishes, reasoning that the food would be nearby. Shadow was sitting calmly in a little pantry that was at the far end of the kitchen. Here Gerry found all that she needed.

While the dog crunched his supper, Gerry sat down at the other end of the kitchen, where, in one corner, was a table, banquettes and a couple of chairs. "Nice," she said aloud, approving the colours. Grey floor, white walls, cabinets and shelves, green upholstery upon which she was sitting, and the table had a natural blond wood finish. Homey but sleek at the same time. A bouquet of a few pink Gerbera daisies in a glass bowl adorned the table.

She heard a mighty lapping that lasted for some time. Then Shadow padded over, sat and stared. "Walk?" she hazarded. He led her to the door. From a black metal hook in the shape of a Labrador's head hung his leash. She clipped it on and they went outside.

There was no way she was going to let him loose as his owners did—what if he failed to obey her and took off towards the road? But he was well trained, did his business, smelling trees and bushes. Gerry wondered if he would be all right alone in the house overnight. Edwina had said he would. "How about if I come over later and take you out again?" she asked him. He took no notice, just kept sniffing around his property.

After a few more minutes, she returned him to his home, gave him a cookie and locked the door. When she got home she rummaged in her gardening shed for a pair of secateurs and cut a rough path through the brambles and wild roses that separated her backyard from Edwina's. Then she went in to her supper.

After eating, she thought she would check on the pool. It was more than half full. She made a mental note to check it again tomorrow morning. The sound of a car arriving at Edwina's made her turn her head. She was a long way away from Edwina's back door, but she thought the person getting out of the car, a snazzy red convertible, was Roald's girlfriend, Andrea.

The woman knocked on the door, then pounded. "Edwina! I know you're in there! Let me in!" Then, as Gerry watched, she reached up to the ledge over the door, obviously looking for the key. Gerry heard Shadow barking.

Baffled, the woman walked over to Edwina's remaining car and peered in. She pounded on the house door again, this time calling, "Roald! Roald! What's going on?" The dog barked more loudly, possibly at the mention of his owner's name.

Gerry really didn't want to be the one to tell the woman that Roald was dead. And it wasn't as if she had any details, either. She stayed where she was, feeling bad, until Andrea got into her car and drove away. The dog barked for a few seconds more.

"Phew!" said Gerry. "This is not good."

For the rest of the evening she watched TV from her sofa, surrounded by cats who seemed willing to exchange the now unneeded warmth of the huge fireplace's hearth for the flickering lights of the electronic one.

At ten, Gerry switched it off and took the newly cleared path to Edwina's. As before, the dog was sitting inside the back door. Gerry hoped he wasn't waiting for the man who was never coming home.

They walked around the yard in the quiet May night. Frogs peeped from the creeks and pools across the road and from the ditches. A nighthawk sent its sonic beeps into the air, searching for clouds of insects. A few mosquitoes buzzed half-heartedly around Gerry's face. She brushed them away. The nights were still too cold, the standing water also still too cold for many of the annoying creatures to have been born.

She and the dog walked down to the lake's edge and from far away heard the ragged pops of fireworks exploding.

She turned her head. She'd forgotten it was a holiday Monday. Maybe if Doug had been there they would have driven to Lovering to watch the show. As it was, only the tops of the largest expanding domes and fountains of colour were visible above the trees. And then they ended and the quiet night returned.

Gerry was up early the next morning, worried about Shadow. She gave her own pets their kibble and meat, and hurried outside. As soon as she stepped on to the lawn and looked towards Edwina's house, she could tell something further was happening.

One of the unmarked cars that had been at the house the previous day—she couldn't remember which, the blue one or the grey—was parked behind the house, and two of the four men in suits who had visited Edwina had returned. They had their backs to Gerry and were looking up at a second-storey window, which was open.

They didn't hear Gerry coming across the lawn, and both turned sharply when she asked, "Can I help you?"

In suits, ties and topcoats, they were dressed conservatively, in a way she associated with television police detectives. One removed his topcoat and draped it over his arm. "Who are you?" he said.

The other larger one took a step towards her. Gerry stepped back. The one who'd first spoken laid a hand on his partner's shoulder and smiled. "We're looking for Roald. Or Edwina."

At first Gerry was nonplussed. If they were police, shouldn't they identify themselves first? And use people's full names? And wouldn't they know Edwina was in jail? Then the penny dropped. Not police. "I don't know where they are. Edwina asked me to care for the dog for a day or two."

The guy still wearing his topcoat took another step forward. "Oh, good," he said. "You can let us in. We, ah, have something to pick up."

Gerry backed up. "I don't think I can do that," she was beginning to say nervously when they all heard the sound of a vehicle arriving at Gerry's. "My friends," she said, turned and began walking briskly back to her place.

When she looked over her shoulder, the calmer guy was talking to the bigger more aggressive one. They got into their car and left.

By now Gerry had reached the thicket. She looked up to her parking pad and saw Lucie and Terry, the renovators.

"Morning, Boss," Terry grinned.

"Your timing is impeccable," Gerry panted. "I've just been ever so slightly menaced by two men over at Edwina Murray's house."

Terry frowned. "Yeah, there were some pretty peculiar guys hanging around when we were working on the house. They gone?"

"I think so. But would you come over there with me while I let the dog out? I feel jumpy."

"Sure. Luce, you start unloading the tools."

"I'm already doing it," came a cranky voice from behind the van. "And I heard everything. Go let the poor dog out for a pee."

"Where's Edwina?" Terry asked as he followed Gerry back to Edwina's house.

"You haven't heard? Roald's dead." Terry let out a long low whistle. Gerry continued, "I don't really know in which circumstances except Edwina said he'd been shot. She's been taken into custody. Yesterday. Thus," she unlocked the door. "The dog."

The dog was sitting in his usual spot and thumped his tail when he saw Terry. Terry seized the dog's head and scrunched his ears. "Who's a good boy? Who's a good Shadow?" The dog yawned and stretched, wagging his tail.

"Well, you certainly get more of a reaction out of him than I do."

Terry shrugged. "He prefers men, I guess. He kind of just tolerates Edwina too. Do you like what we did to the kitchen?" Gerry nodded and fed and watered the dog while he talked. "It was knotty pine cupboards up and down. Nice but dark. We ripped them out and found a buyer for them, so Edwina got some money, then we put this in. It was all to Edwina's specs. She seemed to have had it all thought out. But tell me, why is she being held at the police station?"

"I really don't know. I thought she would just have to identify the body, not spend the night there."

"Unless—" He stopped short.

"What?" By now Shadow had finished gulping his food, had emptied his water bowl and was whining to go out. "We better take the dog." Once outside, following Shadow from tree to tree, she repeated her question. "What were you going to say? You said 'Unless—'"

"Mmm. Well, maybe she's in protective custody. Roald was in with a nasty crowd. If he was murdered—"

Gerry finished what she thought Terry had been about to say. "Maybe they think Edwina will tell on the bad guys."

"Yeah," he said doubtfully. "What I was going to say, is maybe Edwina knows where something is. Something Roald took or had that he shouldn't have."

They both turned to look at the empty house. "Something in there," Gerry said. "Those guys that just left were looking up at that open window."

"Am I the only one ready to get to work here today?" Lucie stood, hands on hips, on Gerry's side of the thicket.

Terry and Gerry looked sheepishly at each other.

"Will you tell her or will I?" Gerry asked.

"I will. Coming, Mother," he called. As Lucie stomped back towards the van, he smiled at Gerry. "She hates when I call her Mother."

After Gerry returned Shadow to his home, she went upstairs, closed and locked the window and checked all the others. The dog followed her from room to room. Her last glimpse of him when she locked the back door was of him turning away and padding slowly down the hallway.

PART 3

HOME TO ROOST

Lovey couldn't find Melancholy. His paws twitched in his sleep. His lips were tense and lifted to reveal his fangs. He woke with a start as he heard her howl. He looked toward the foot of the bed where she liked to sleep, nearest the door, so she could escape if the terrors came too close. Gone. He stretched, reluctantly left his warm spot snuggled into the girl's back and dropped to the floor. He sat on the landing outside the girl's bedroom door while he got his bearings.

The house sighed, filled with busy spirits, coming and going. They went up and down the stairs by ones and twos: an older man and a middle-aged woman, murmuring together in apparent anguish; two younger men in shirtsleeves, boys really, one with a noticeable limp, who climbed the staircase slowly and descended quickly, tears on their cheeks; and assorted others, mostly women in long dresses who came in through the front door and didn't stay long, but departed shaking their heads.

Melancholy uttered another long drawn out howl. Now Lovey knew where she was. He trotted down the hall to another bedroom, where usually a group of four cats took their rest.

The four cats were there but not on the bed. Instead they crouched with Melancholy in front of the fireplace in which smoke swirled from a ghostly fire. Lovey took his spot alongside Melancholy, feeling her lifted fur touch his.

In the bed a young woman gasped for breath. The middle-aged woman knelt by the bed, her head bowed, hands clasped in front of her.

The older man came into the room holding a little yellow piece of paper. He held it out to the woman who took it with trembling fingers. Her ashen face became white bone with two staring, hollow eyes. She crumpled the paper and with a cry hurled it into the fire. The burning paper exuded a yellow vapour that filled the room. Lovey felt his eye sting.

The woman looked up at the man and shook her head, pointing at the gasping figure in the bed. The man sank to his knees on the other side of the bed and the couple's hands met over her body as the young woman breathed her last.

As the cats watched, an even mistier version of the young woman sat up, left the sad couple still kneeling, and left the room. Melancholy trotted after her. Lovey followed Melancholy.

The girl wafted down the stairs, pausing to lightly touch the two boys who ran up the stairs towards her room, from where a sound of lamentation came. She looked after them as they stumbled unseeing past her.

She slipped through the front door of the house. Melancholy and Lovey darted to the cat flap at the back of the house and entered the night.

A half-moon shone its limited glow over the garden. The lake shimmered. The cats took their time. There was no rush. They knew where she'd go.

They crept to the parking pad and stopped next to one of the car's rear wheels.

She stood by the road, her nightdress fluttering as she turned first this way, then that.

11

Tell me what you would have me to say, for I am
cluttered out of my senses. (1685)

Gerry reached down, twisted and yanked. The ruby red stalk released easily. She repeated the motion seven more times before straightening. She looked at her harvest with satisfaction. But she'd forgotten to bring a knife. She snapped off the big leaves and dropped them near the plant. The rhubarb showed no sign of surrendering. If only all we needed was rhubarb, she thought. We'd be all set. She took her bounty to the kitchen.

As she washed and sliced the rhubarb, she listened for the sounds of Lucie and Terry at work. It was quiet right now. Before there had been the thuds of sledgehammers through drywall, and Lucie's high-pitched continuous exasperated-sounding commentary punctuated by Terry's lower rumbles and laughs. They seemed to work well as a team.

When the dust started to rise, settling on the painters' tarps spread over the dining room carpet and furniture, Gerry and any cats who weren't already put off by the loud noises backed away. That's when she thought of using up some of the rhubarb to make a cake.

Rhubarb Coffee Cake, the recipe said. It had been copied in Aunt Maggie's hand onto an index card. A straightforward cake, but with two to four cups of chopped rhubarb folded into the batter at the last minute. The sugar was also given a variable amount, and Gerry reasoned that this was supposed to be linked to how much sour rhubarb she decided to use. A flexible recipe that depended on the canniness of the cook. As the sugar-fruit ratio was not one to one, she dithered for a moment until she figured it out. She decided three cups rhubarb to one and a quarter cups of sugar.

Once the cake was in the oven, she made coffee and took it, three mugs and cream and sugar into the dining room. The reason for the relative silence was revealed.

The alcove and its shelves were gone. Lucie was snapping large chunks of broken drywall into smaller pieces and stuffing them into giant garbage bags. "I like to clean up as we go," she explained.

Gerry nodded. "Like in the kitchen."

"Exactly." Lucie swept dust from the floor into a pan. She jerked her head towards the opening in the wall. "Have a peek."

Gerry moved closer, rested her hands on the rough edges on either side and leaned in. Terry, rummaging in the far end of the space, looked up. "Seems like you got yourself a store," he cheerfully informed her.

Empty wooden crates were stacked along one wall. Barrels were perched on top of the boxes. A little window in the lake side wall had been boarded up. Stacks of newspapers were under a long narrow counter on the opposite wall. Above the counter were numerous pigeonholes. And at the end of the space, where Terry stood, was an old-fashioned desk with a rolled-down top and a chair. Terry grinned. "Cool, eh?"

"Wow." Gerry breathed the word out slowly. "This is amazing. Don't move anything until I've had a chance to look at it, okay?"

Lucie spoke from behind her. "Yep. That's what we figured you'd say. We'll finish tidying and go work on the bamboo room."

"That would be great. It's the room I'm most anxious about, because of the bamboo wall covering. I'd love to use it for my art studio all year round."

"We'll be careful," Lucie assured her. "Terry, stop poking around and come out here. You can carry these bags outside." Terry exited the store rolling his eyes.

"Have a coffee?" Gerry suggested, indicating the tray.

"Don't mind if I do." Terry smiled. "Thanks." He and Lucie finished with the bags and took their coffees into the bamboo room.

"No cats in there," Gerry called after them. The old wall covering had to be protected from claws. Slightly rough-textured, and somewhat bark-like, it would make the perfect cat scratching material.

She got out the much-repaired old vacuum cleaner and began on the area outside the store. Then she swept the inside more carefully than Lucie had, lifting things and peering behind them, removing cobwebs from the ceiling and inspecting the covered window more closely. She passed a rag over the desk and discovered it was locked. When she was sure there were no small objects on the floor that might get sucked into the vacuum, she thoroughly cleaned the store, mercilessly sucking up years of spiderwebs along with their present and past occupants.

She stepped back into the dining room, poured herself a coffee and sat down on one of the chairs, first removing Harley, the large black and white cat who was sitting there. His brother, Kitty-Cat, who Gerry always wished had been called Davidson, also belonging to the species *Cattus immensus*, sat on the next chair over.

Her lap was barely large enough for the cat, and once he'd circled and kneaded and resettled, she had to cup her left hand around him so he wouldn't slip off. She reached over to pet Kitty-Cat. What a funny life I'm having, she thought. Cats and hidden rooms and rhubarb. "Aagh! The cake!"

She stood, letting Harley slide gently onto the rug, and ran to the kitchen. The smell was enticing. The cake, crusty brown from the brown sugar, butter and cinnamon in the streusel topping, looked done. She got out a wooden toothpick and inserted it into the centre. It was wet with batter when she pulled it out. Huh. Cooked on top but not inside. What would Prudence do? Gerry ripped a piece of tinfoil from its roll and loosely covered the cake. Another fifteen minutes? She set the timer, wondering why she hadn't done that in the first place. After all, the recipe did say bake fifty to sixty minutes. She could have easily wandered off outside and had a burnt mess. Wandered off outside…there was something she was supposed to do… For the second time in five minutes she shouted "Aagh!" and dashed outside.

The pool was full. Thankful she hadn't flooded the backyard (not that it would have mattered so close to the lake, but it would have meant wasting water), she shut off the hose and dragged it back to the carport where she coiled it. She was back inside loitering near the oven when she looked up to see a bedraggled-looking Edwina Murray pass in front of the kitchen window. There came a timid knock.

Gerry flung open the door. "Oh, you poor thing. Come in, come in. I just made coffee. And there'll be cake to go with it soon. I hope. Have you ever made rhubarb cake?"

Edwina shook her head. Gerry, who realized she was just chattering to fill the empty space, continued, "It says bake for an hour. I've never had to bake a cake for that long." She paused for breath.

"Thanks for looking after Shadow," Edwina said, still standing outside. "I won't come in. I need—" She shuddered. "I need to wash. I just wanted you to know I'm home."

"Oh, okay. But you should know two guys, the two that visited you a few days ago, on the weekend, were back this morning. Not the cops, the other ones."

Edwina turned even more pale, which didn't seem possible, and sagged, putting out a hand to the doorframe for support.

"I really think you should come inside," Gerry said kindly. "A snack will do you good."

"I couldn't eat when I was…was…there!" Edwina whimpered. She stepped up into the porch and Gerry led her to the living room sofa.

"There, there, you just rest and I'll make you a sandwich." Edwina lay down and Gerry covered her with the throw, then made a lettuce, tomato and cheese sandwich. When she took it to Edwina, the woman was asleep.

"Well," said Gerry to Bob and Mother who were hovering. "What a peculiar day!" She wrapped the sandwich, took the cake out of the oven and went to see what Lucie and Terry were doing.

What they were doing was looking ruefully at a long strip of the bamboo wall covering which they'd partially removed from the wall. "Oh no!" Gerry wailed.

Lucie immediately moved into damage control mode. "We'll stick it back on, no problem, but what it means is that, for this room at least, we'll have to work from the outside."

"Can you do that?" Gerry wondered.

"Sure," Terry replied. "Remove the outside siding, which is wood, and easy to repair; insulate; replace siding. May just do the whole house that way, seeing as we'll have to rent scaffolding. No disturbance inside. Better for you."

"And," said Lucie, "the weather forecast for the next few days is good. So we should be able to do quite a lot before it rains."

"Even then," Terry reassured, "we can cover it with tarps. Okay?"

"Okay," Gerry agreed.

"We're going to eat lunch and then we'll get going. We need to get the scaffold, so that will take a few hours."

"Whatever you have to do. Just make sure that at the end of it all, I can use the room in winter."

"You got it." Terry smiled and cheekily saluted. This time it was Lucie who rolled her eyes.

Gerry made another sandwich and ate it on the back porch while Edwina slumbered on. Gerry watched Terry and Lucie sitting at her picnic table on the lawn as they enjoyed the view and ate. She returned to reading *Dangerous to Know*.

The plot hinged (as she'd supposed from the book's cover) on the key that may or may not have been dropped on purpose for the heroine to find. It was complicated. If the man who dropped it meant her to have it, was it because he needed her help or was he trying to trap or trick her? It didn't help that the heroine had a crush on the man. The reader was kept guessing: is he a good guy or not? It wasn't until the very last page that Gerry found out.

She looked up with a sigh as she closed the book. To her astonishment, much of the afternoon was behind her. Her workers had left and not returned. She assumed they couldn't begin until the scaffolding was in place. She'd enjoyed Edwina's book. It had been a compelling read. Then she remembered. "Edwina!" she cried. She rushed into the living room where she'd left her but Edwina was gone.

12

Clots or clutters of congealed blood. (1611)

Gerry thought for a moment, then fed the cats. As twenty furry little bodies churned in the feeding area on the kitchen floor and the smell of tinned cat food rose nauseatingly into the air, she sighed. This was now her life. And would be for the immediate future, as two-thirds of the cats were young or middle-aged.

She cut a good-sized chunk of the now cooled rhubarb cake and ate it. Very delicious. Then she cut another larger chunk and wrapped it. She put the rest of the cake away in an upper cupboard (after all, who knew what hungry cats might nibble on?) and let herself out the side door. She walked through the newly cleared path to Edwina's house and knocked on the back door.

A voice from above quietly called, "Gerry!"

Gerry looked up. Edwina, with a towel around her head, was leaning out an upstairs window.

"I brought back your key," Gerry said, "and some cake."

"Let yourself in. I'm coming down." The head disappeared.

Gerry entered the house and waited. Edwina came into the hallway and locked the door. She seemed to have recovered some of her poise.

"Feel better?" Gerry asked kindly.

"Yes, I do, thanks." Edwina even managed a smile.

"Rhubarb cake," Gerry said, handing it over.

"Thank you. Will you stay?" Gerry nodded. "I'll just get dressed. Look around, if you want, and see what you think of Lucie and Terry's work." She went back upstairs.

Shadow came out of the kitchen and followed Gerry as she toured the downstairs.

The layout seemed a bit strange to her. To one side of the front door was a blocky wooden staircase with open stairs and railings. It turned every six steps as it made a squared-off spiral ascent. The entranceway just kind of spilled out into the living area. You walked down a step to the left to sofas and a large stone open fireplace and up a step on the right to a dining area.

Gerry wandered over past the fireplace to an open doorway. Edwina's study, she supposed, as the furniture was comprised of a large desk with a computer, files and papers scattered on the rest of the desk's surface, and several bookcases. A vase of daffodils on a windowsill completed the image of a serene workspace for a successful author.

She re-entered the living room, passing the staircase on her right, and entered a room similar in size to Edwina's office that she immediately identified as being Roald's den. A pool table dominated the room. There was just enough room left for a couple of comfy leather armchairs, a bar, and a table between the armchairs where Gerry could see and smell the remains of a couple of cigars and a small collection of pipes.

Shadow lay down on a small rug between the chairs and sighed. Gerry knelt down and stroked his head. "Ah, I'm sorry, fella, I'm sorry."

"He's pining, of course," Edwina said from the doorway. She'd changed into loose jeans with a sweatshirt and left her wet hair to air dry. She looked a lot younger that way. "But he's still eating. So I guess he'll recover. What do you think of the renovation?"

Gerry gulped. She'd been in the house pre-Edwina on a few occasions, but only when it was unoccupied. She'd either been chasing her cat Bob from room to room or being asked by the police to identify a man's dead body in the kitchen. "I seem to remember the downstairs was several smaller rooms." She paused by the staircase. "And this was just an ordinary staircase going straight up." She paused. "And it was over here, I think."

Edwina nodded. "I didn't like it and it had to be moved in order to have an open-space living area. I designed this staircase after an Arts and Crafts one I saw in a house in Scotland."

"Oh," said Gerry politely. "It is very Arts and Crafts. Yes. So what did Lucie and Terry do? The staircase?"

"Oh no. I had that built off site by timber craftsmen. Lucie and Terry tore out the interior walls, insulated and replastered. They did the kitchen too. Come, I'll make tea."

Gerry followed. She was liking this new, more confident Edwina, but wondering what they'd find to talk about besides the house. Edwina put on the kettle and they sat in the booth in the corner of the kitchen. "Well," Gerry said brightly, "This is nice."

Edwina gave her a look. "I can tell you're uneasy. Do you think I murdered my husband?"

Gerry's jaw dropped. "Eh!?" was all she could manage.

Edwina put one elbow on the table and propped her face in her cupped hand. "Because the police think so. It's so interesting. My husband has been murdered. Naturally they suspect me. The spouse is one of the people most likely to have done it. The interesting part is that I write murder mysteries." The kettle whistled.

Edwina seemed to have forgotten about Gerry's cake and Gerry didn't like to remind her. Edwina shook some cookies out of a bag onto a plate. While the tea steeped, she stared out the kitchen window.

Gerry took a deep breath. "While I hardly know you," she began, "I was not suspicious that you might have killed Roald. No. I thought you being with the police was more likely to have something to do with those two guys who visited you and then returned when you were...away." She thought for a moment. "But they were asking for Roald—or you—when he was already dead. So they didn't know he was dead. And I didn't tell them."

Edwina brought the tea and cookies to the table. Her composure had diminished. "Loan sharks. I think. Anyway, people Roald owed money to. They wouldn't kill him as long as they thought he could get the money from me. They must know Roald's dead by now. And," she added grimly, "they must know I'm suspected."

"Er, why exactly are you suspected?" Gerry asked as delicately as she could.

"Because there was blood in my car trunk, for one thing," Edwina said gloomily.

Gerry started and her eyes opened wide under raised brows.

"Oh, no!" Edwina assured her. "Last week I took Shadow for a good long run on that trail that leads into the fields across from the big church in Lovering."

Gerry nodded. She knew the spot. Lovering was probably unique in that it boasted not one but two Anglican churches. It also had two United churches and the Roman Catholic church, which was at the centre of the village. A god-fearing group of settlers had left their various countries of origin and made their mark locally in the times past when people expected to be able to walk to church. "That's St. Martin's Church," she said.

Edwina continued, "He went on ahead of me and disappeared. I walked back to the parking lot where the trail starts. He always comes eventually. Sure enough, he reappeared with a dead squirrel in his mouth and dropped it next to the car. Well, I couldn't just leave it there. Church goers park there when their parking lot is full. And there wasn't a garbage can. So I picked it up and put it in the trunk. When I got home I wrapped it in newspaper and put it into the garbage. All of which—" She paused and sipped her tea. "I told the police."

Gerry continued for her. "But they thought it was Roald's blood and took you and the car into custody until they checked for his blood type. Well, I suppose the technicians can tell it's not human blood right away."

Edwina nodded. "You'd think so, wouldn't you? But apparently not. They have to use special tests and that takes time. And of course my garbage was picked up last week so I can't produce the squirrel. As I understand it, the blood in my car trunk is both for and against me being the murderer. I know it's squirrel blood; they don't. They've sent a sample to a lab for further testing, but who knows how long that will take? In the meantime I shall do my own research."

Gerry looked at her doubtfully. Edwina seemed to see the problem of the bloodstain as an intellectual one, soon to be solved. "I hope you're right." She took a store-bought chocolate chip cookie from the plate and dunked it in her tea. Unlike Prudence, who turned her nose up at such products, Gerry wasn't fussy. "But until then—"

Edwina likewise chomped on a cookie. "Until then, I'm their number one suspect. Plus, there's the gun." Gerry blinked. Edwina continued calmly, "He was shot and rolled over the cliff behind that same church. Wound up on the railway tracks. The engineer found him when he was bringing the cars for the first train of the day."

Gerry said slowly, "That's terrible. I think I may know that engineer. That puts you near where the body was found."

Edwina waved her hand impatiently. "But a week earlier."

"Still, you knew the place." Gerry paused as if just then registering what else Edwina had said. "The police have the gun?"

Edwina nodded. "Roald had one. A handgun of some kind. I told him to keep it away from me. I can find all I need to know about guns for my books on the internet. I don't need to handle one."

"And was he shot with his own gun?" Gerry asked in horrified tones.

Edwina shrugged. "Perhaps. Again, those test results aren't immediately available. It's more where the gun was found."

Gerry waited.

"Under his car," Edwina stated in a puzzled voice. "In my driveway."

"But anybody could have put it there," Gerry said indignantly.

"That's what I said. I asked them if they really thought I was stupid enough to leave a gun I'd just killed my husband with under one of our cars. They said maybe I was confused or upset. Or maybe I dropped it accidentally. As if."

"How did you not see it?"

"Well, since he's been gone, I haven't used either of the cars. And we have a circular driveway. You can't pass the car ahead of you. We just used either of the cars, really, whichever one was in front, rather than back out onto the road. That little hill makes it tricky. You can't see."

"So someone is trying to set you up for his murder," Gerry said slowly.

"I guess. What else could it be? Anyway, we still don't know if Roald's gun was even the one used to shoot him."

Gerry leaned forward. "Do you have names for the two guys, the loan sharks?"

"The police asked that too. Just first names. Or rather, name. The smaller one called the big one Micky. Or Mikey. No, Micky. I could use them in one of my books."

Gerry could see how Edwina's vagueness might seem like prevarication to the police. "Well, whatever his name is, he seemed pretty aggressive to me."

Edwina looked at her. "He did, didn't he? Of course they wanted money. I said I wasn't responsible for Roald's debts. I said, if they wanted to, they could take me to court."

Gerry grinned. "I bet they didn't like that!"

Edwina grinned back. "No, they didn't." Then her smile faded. "But they said they'd be back."

"Well, as I told you earlier, they did come back and I talked to them. I assume they know Roald's dead now. Either way, I don't think they'll bother you again."

"Either way?"

"Yeah. If they killed him, they're probably far away by now. And if they didn't and their 'business' is illegal, they know the police will be sniffing around until they find the murderer. So they'll still make themselves scarce."

"You know, I think you're right. The logic holds up." She dropped her head into her hands, covering her eyes. "It's all my own fault," she groaned. "If I hadn't been such a wimp— If I'd just divorced him and somehow paid him off, none of this would be happening to me. Or him."

"Maybe," Gerry said. "But it's no good thinking that now."

Edwina shivered and stood. "I feel better. Thank you for coming, Gerry. I've got to get back to work."

As Gerry walked back to her house she wondered if that work included looking up how to tell squirrel from human blood. Probably.

She checked her answering machine. The light was blinking. "Gerry, it's Judy. Call me." She dialled Judith Parsley's number at home. No answer. Then she remembered that, it being Tuesday and the *Herald* having to go to the printers the following night, Judy and her dad were probably still at work. She was correct.

"*Lovering Herald.* Judy here. May I help you?"

"Judy, it's me, Gerry. You called?"

"Oh, hi, Gerry. Just a sec." There was a rustling of papers. "I found another mention of a death in your family. In 1915. Mary Anne Coneybear. Do you know who she is?"

"Yes. She was one of my great-aunts."

"Oh. Okay. Well, it says she died of a fever at home on May 27, 1915. About a month or so after her brother was killed at Ypres. I'm afraid there's nothing about the store, either being open or closed."

"Thanks, Judy. That's nice of you to have kept looking in your archives. But you'll never guess what. We found the actual store inside the house here. Behind a wall in the dining room. You'll have to come see it. It's like a time capsule."

"Oo! Exciting! Maybe I could do a little piece on it for the paper."

"Great. Meanwhile, I think I should start looking through the family papers for the history of the store. It must be documented somewhere."

"All right. I'll call you in a couple of days."

"'Bye, Judy." Gerry hung up. She was full of cake and cookies. She put another frozen lasagne (good thing she'd bought a few) in the oven. Perhaps in an hour when it was ready, she'd be hungry.

She walked around the house, checking the cats. Most of them seemed relaxed. She passed into the foyer and June's diorama caught her eye. She did a double take.

Of course! June was seeing something that had existed in the past and was reproducing it in the present! It had happened a few months ago and was happening again! The diorama was probably a pretty accurate rendition of what the hundred-year-old store at The Maples had looked like.

She looked more closely at the two little figures. The male was dressed all in beige; the female wore a mauve dress. Could they be her relatives?

She ran to get her family tree, scattering a few cats who were nearby. She looked for the year 1915. Mary Anne and her younger brother Alfred both died that year. And he was in the army. She ran back to the foyer.

The boy was in beige, but June hadn't seen him clearly enough to make his clothes those of a soldier. Yet the two cats looking at the two humans were unmistakably Lightning and Seymour. "Well, she *knows* them," Gerry said aloud. "But she's only *feeling* the boy and the girl. Amazing."

Her brain raced as she ate her supper. How all this was going to be relevant, she couldn't see. After all, they'd never figured out why June had been drawing an assembly of people, most of them Gerry and Prudence's relations, a few months earlier. A group of people dressed in old-fashioned clothing standing on Gerry's back lawn. Also included in the drawing, one of Gerry's cats—Jay the kitten. She almost choked. Jay, who had later dug up a briefcase of cash in Gerry's garden under the apple tree. Did that mean Lightning and Seymour were linked to the finding of the store in some way?

Then she shrugged. June just picks up on these things, she reasoned. They don't have to *mean* anything. Probably best to ask Judy not to mention the diorama in her article. If she notices it. And if she does write an article. I wouldn't want to embarrass June.

With all these thoughts in her head, and with all that was going on with Edwina next door, Gerry decided what she needed was a nice relaxing bath. And a book. She found *Purple Angel* and read until the bathwater turned cold.

13

It killith them...by congealing and cluttering their blood. (1601)

Our minister is a tall man with a kind expression. He has two churches, one near where I live at one end of Lovering with my mother and father and brother and sister, and one further away, past the other side of the village.

(I should say I also live with my cats. First there was Puff but she ran away. Now we have Mr. Puff and Snickerdoodle. Mr. Puff is named for the first Puff (who was a girl) and is black; and Snickerdoodle is named after my favourite cookies. She has a pale cream undercoat with longer ginger hairs on top.

In case you don't know, snickerdoodles are lovely. Like sugar cookies but you roll the dough into a ball, then roll that in a bowl of cinnamon sugar. The balls spread out in the oven.

My brother Gerry says I should put in a closing bracket and get back to the minister. So here it is: the bracket, I mean, then the minister.)

The minister's name is Mr. Postlethwaite. My brother says there is no easy way to pronounce this. Paw then stealth then wait. This makes it seem almost like a cat name. Paw—obvious. Stealth, which I have just looked up, is: 'the act or action of proceeding furtively, secretly, or imperceptibly.' (I also had to look up furtively and imperceptibly but you probably already know what they mean. If you don't, I recommend a big fat dictionary like the one my father keeps on his desk.) And cats are good at waiting. Waiting for a bird or mouse to come closer. Not so good at waiting for their suppers when they yowl.

Mr. P. (the minister, not my cat) has a wife and four daughters. Their names are Sarah, Anne, Jane and Beulah and they are all grown-up ladies. They live with their parents in the big old house next to the church the farthest away from my church.

I feel sorry for Beulah. It is such a strange name compared to her sisters'. I might name one of my cats, a future cat, Beulah, but cat names are different from human names. They don't have to be a family name like Margaret—my name—is. There have been a few Margarets in the Coneybear family. I am named for my Great-Aunt Margie.

Mr. Postlethwaite is very old, older than Dad. This means he was the right age to fight in the Great War, which is what my parents call the First World War. To be that age wasn't very good for men. There is a big plaque in our church with a long list of the names of the men who died in it. My father's brother Alfred died in 1915 at somewhere called Ypres, which my brother says is another impossible to pronounce word. He gave me the French pronunciation—Eepruh—and the English— Wipers. As Ypres is in Belgium, next to France, I will pronounce it the French way. The English way sounds funnier though.

But Ypres was not a fun place for Canadian soldiers. Mr. Postlethwaite was there. He was an army chaplain, which is like being a minister only you don't get a house. He wasn't wounded. But my mother and father sometimes exchange a look when Mr. Postlethwaite is here for tea, stops talking and just stares blankly at the air in front of him. I know what my parents' look means. They also exchange it when I do or say something they don't like. It means "We will discuss this later."

(I hope I have included enough punctuation in this essay. It wasn't easy but I think I found a place for everything except a colon. No, there is one colon.)

Gerry yawned and stretched. She closed the exercise book in which her Aunt Maggie had written her elementary school compositions, got up and made another cup of coffee. The day had begun with the usual cat-related chores, then she'd decided, as she was on vacation, to play around with her idea for making a book for children using her aunt's stories accompanied by illustrations of Lovering as it had used to be.

"The Minister Who Wasn't There" was dated from 1959, when her aunt would have been about ten or eleven years old. Grade five or grade six. It was the most coherent and the longest of the stories. But how could it be illustrated? She grabbed some paper and sketched the two cats at the beginning of the story— Mr. Puff and Snickerdoodle—and the four minister's daughters how she imagined they might have been dressed in the fifties—in swirling skirts, little sweaters and saddle shoes. She gave Beulah a pair of glasses.

She hummed as she worked and the ideas began to flow. She added a sketch of the church near her house—St. Anne's— and of the plaque she'd read many times, on one of the church's interior walls; a military chaplain kneeling over a fallen soldier in a trench as shells burst overhead and other men went over the top; a middle-aged man holding a teacup, staring past the perplexed couple sitting opposite.

"There!" She looked at the collection of sketches. She had enough. For this story anyway.

Lucie and Terry had arrived that morning and assembled their scaffolding at the side of the house next to the bamboo room. Gerry had tried to ignore the sound of first the truck delivering the scaffolding and then the subsequent sound of another truck dropping off the rolls of rockwool. Then came the workers' muffled voices as they put together the pipes and platform and began prying off the house's cladding.

As usual, her work had eventually absorbed her, so that now when she heard nothing outside and her stomach audibly reminded her of its existence, she remembered the sandwich she'd made for Edwina, ate it quickly, then walked outside to observe the work site. She found Lucie and Terry in folding camping chairs, eating their lunch under the apple tree.

Lucie smiled. "Lovely garden. Lovely place to eat lunch."

Gerry turned to survey the house. The cladding was off and the frame stood exposed. Thin slats of wood were all that protected her precious bamboo room from the elements. The house felt vulnerable to her and, by extension, so did she herself.

"How long? To do this wall, I mean."

Lucie replied. "It's the set-up that's a time-suck: the scaffolding, taking the siding off carefully. We only split one piece." She paused as if expecting praise, then seemed to sense Gerry's tension. "It's all right, you know. We've done this before. The house can take it."

Gerry nodded. "It makes me nervous, as if I'm disturbing something."

"You're adding to the house's longevity, if anything," Terry reassured her. "We'll lay the rockwool today and throw as much siding back on as we can." He got up and walked to a plastic tarp, laid on the ground. "Here, look at this."

Gerry walked over and looked down. Layers of old newspapers, some half-rotted, rested on the tarp. A few stones kept them in place.

Lucie joined them. "We usually save some in case the owners are interested in history. Wait a sec." She dug into a pocket of her overalls and held several small objects out to Gerry. "Square-headed nails. Hundred, hundred and fifty years old. Cool, eh?"

Gerry took the nails, some rusty, some snapped in two, into her hands. "Very cool. Why are they square?"

Lucie replied. "Would've been made by hand. By a blacksmith. Banged out on his forge. I'd wear gloves if and when you handle the papers. Mouse poop."

Gerry went to get gardening gloves and put the square-headed nails on a shelf in the potting shed next to the remaining catnip plants. As usual, Lightning and Seymour were sitting by the shed's door next to a tub of geraniums. They were dozing, it seemed. Gerry had grown so used to seeing them there that she didn't comment on it. If that's where they wanted to sit, it was fine by her.

Lucie and Terry were unrolling and measuring strips of rockwool when she returned to get a stack of newspapers. So they wouldn't blow away, she took them onto the back porch and began carefully flipping through them.

They were from an earlier time period than the papers she and Judy had perused together, presumably before the *Lovering Herald* had ever existed. After a quick glance, she ascertained she was looking at records from the second half of the nineteenth century. Many of the papers were in French, a language Gerry had little knowledge of.

There could be no question of preserving them; many crumbled as Gerry tried to separate them from the stack. She thought for a moment, then went and got paper and pen. She worked through the stack, noting the name of the paper and the date it was published, if that was visible, along with a brief summary of what that sheet contained.

What they contained, she thought, as the afternoon went by, was life.

The news of the day, which seemed mostly political; local news of church activity, which it seemed was one of the few outlets for social life; family news: births, deaths, engagements, marriages; and the accidents: fires, drownings, a collision involving horses; news of the loggers, poling log booms down the Ottawa River.

That last article made Gerry sit back and harvest a memory. Not her own, but something her father had told her about.

How, when he was young and playing along the river's edge, tugboats would drag booms of wood—pine axed north of Ottawa and held together by a necklace of chained logs—south to the sawmills and pulp factories of the St. Lawrence River. How he'd imagined being one of those tugboat operators. And how the booms had eventually stopped; their transportation replaced by truck and train; the river dammed.

For just a second, Gerry felt a little closer to the history of the river, saw its place in the history of her family, the importance of the location of her house. "Along the river," she murmured, "the old road. And the store, of course, where boats could deliver goods, even people."

She continued turning the pages of the old newspapers until Terry and Lucie came to say goodbye for the day. "I covered the other papers in case you want to save them," Terry called from the lawn.

"Thank you," Gerry called back. "See you tomorrow." She fed the cats. She thought for a moment, got out her little knapsack and put a few things in it. Then, after putting on her swimming shoes and while the cats were enjoying their suppers, she quietly let herself out.

The river was calm, at least along the shore, and she knew she'd be safe as long as she kept close in near land.

The spring thaw had been long and gradual, with few reports of flooding, but she could see by how much of the backyards of low-lying properties (including her own) were inundated that the water level was high.

She had a supper appointment at the Lovering Yacht Club, but was very early, so decided to make this a long canoe trip. She passed the wooded point halfway between The Maples and the club, noting how the water got a bit choppy off the point. Rocks underwater, she guessed. She proceeded carefully, looking at the water's surface and paddling slowly.

After the point, the land curved gently to the public beach where a few dogs and children played, past the public wharf, and so to the yacht club. She paddled past its breakwater, its collection of boats, where a few people were doing mysterious boaty things aboard their vessels, a few sheds, and the clubhouse proper, to the beach where she planned to land, not now, but later.

Here too a few parents lolled in chairs watching their kids splash at the edge of the water or build sandcastles. It was still too cold for swimming. Gerry, who'd dressed in slacks and a light jacket, was sweating from her paddling. But every time she paused, the current, bent on sweeping everything south and east toward the St. Lawrence and the sea, pushed her tiny craft back towards her house.

After the yacht club she noticed the landscape changing. Lovering rose higher, more trees climbed cliffs, fewer houses were visible.

She knew enough geography to be able to explain this rise. The whole plain through which the Ottawa River passed had been gouged by a glacier. The higher part of Lovering must be founded on harder rock that had resisted the glacier's grinding motion.

She had a moment's reflection that she was glad her property was at the relatively lower end of Lovering, nestled close to the river. On the other hand, the householders up here on the heights, a hundred or more feet above her little canoe, must enjoy different and farther views than she did.

She was too far below the level of the road to hear cars. The birds around her—ducks and geese floating; swallows darting swiftly down from the cliff side trees to swoop over the water— made their small sounds. Away in the distance to the south she heard the warning call of a train's horn. Short, short, long, short. The whistle signal for coming to a crossing.

Maybe that's Gordon, she thought, coming home for the day. I wonder what June's baked for his dessert tonight. She checked her watch. Yup. Six-thirty. The last train to Lovering was approaching. She paddled on.

And then the trees parted and the railway tracks were visible, low down the cliff, hugging the rocky shore. She looked up and could just barely make out the benches she knew were set on the lawn behind St. Martin's Church.

She looked back at the tracks. This, then, was where Roald's body had been found. But had he been killed down on the tracks or up in the churchyard and then flung down the cliff? Edwina had said up in the churchyard. Maybe the police had found a lot of blood up there. But he could have been killed elsewhere. Did it matter where? Surely all that mattered was who had done it.

She had no clues—apart from the gun and blood at Edwina's— just plenty of suspects. The wife, the debt collectors, the girlfriend. She mulled over their various motives as she made her way back to the yacht club.

Edwina stood to gain nothing by Roald's death, but to keep a great deal: her house and other property. And she gained one huge intangible—her independence from a money-sucking, unfaithful husband.

The debt collectors had a weak motive. Surely, if they knew their trade, killing a client was the wrong move. They'd have no further hope of collecting, though they had tried extracting money from Edwina when they thought Roald was still alive. But what if Roald's death was meant as a warning? To other deadbeats. Gerry's brain assessed this theory and liked it. But it would indicate a breathtaking ruthlessness on their part. What if Roald had otherwise transgressed against them—gone beyond welching on a debt? Had he betrayed somebody? Some thing?

She quickly passed over the girlfriend, Andrea. Why kill her lover? Gerry couldn't think of a good reason unless it had been done accidentally or in a fit of rage. And would Andrea have had the strength to load Roald's body into the trunk of a car, then drag it to the cliff and throw it away? Would Edwina, for that matter? Roald had been a big, heavy man. Gerry doubted if either woman could have done it. But desperate people did unusual things.

She remembered the woman and the man she'd seen in Edwina's yard the day she, Gerry, took the ferry. Could they have been Andrea and somebody else, not Roald? Another potential murderer? The yellow car, she mused. Days later, had Roald been killed at his own house and his body put into one of his own cars for disposal? Gerry felt she was close to a possible version of the truth.

She also remembered Andrea banging on Roald and Edwina's empty house's door after Roald had been killed. Gerry stopped paddling as she further remembered Andrea looking in the remaining car's window. That's when she could have dropped the gun! And kicked it under the car! Accidentally or on purpose. No, wait. The gun had already been found by the police at that moment in time. Hadn't it?

The canoe drifted close to shore where overhanging branches had snagged a large dead tree. Gerry came to her senses when the canoe bumped the log and one of the branches became entangled in her hair. "Sorry," she said to the log, and steered her canoe back into the river.

As she reapplied herself, she remembered with disappointment that both the gangsters had also been near the car or cars in Edwina's driveway. And Edwina, it must be confessed, was so vague sometimes that Gerry could almost believe her capable of dropping a murder weapon in error if she was confused or distracted enough. Almost believe it.

Gerry suspected that when it came to the real world, Edwina was perfectly capable of coping. Hadn't she said she had retirement savings? And she'd had enough money to refurbish the house she'd inherited, though she could have also received a cash bequest from her great-great-cousin's estate. And Terry had said Edwina seemed to have made her plans for the house far in advance of when she took possession.

So any of the suspects could have dropped the gun. And it wasn't even certain that Roald's gun had been the one used to kill him.

As she approached the yacht club, she checked her watch again. Almost seven. Good. She was hungry.

She allowed the canoe to drift close to the little beach at the yacht club, hopped into the cold water and dragged her craft up onto the sand. She deposited her life jacket and wet shoes inside, got her knapsack and headed toward the clubhouse, a low dark wooden building with wraparound verandas on the three sides that had river views. She entered on the fourth side, pausing only in the vestibule to dust off her feet and slip on socks and loafers. She took a deep breath and passed through the yacht club doors.

14

…with a tumult of syllables and clutter upon their lips. (1748)

"Guest of Mary Petherbridge?" Gerry tentatively queried the young woman standing at the dining room entrance.

The club's interior was divided into two large rooms with high ceilings. The one whose entrance she was hovering near contained big round tables with captain's chairs. It had good views of the lake. The hubbub of voices indicated that happy hour was well on its way. But there was no sign of Mary.

"Right this way," the hostess graciously said. Gerry followed her to a set of double doors that opened into a second room. Same chairs and tables, but this room contained the bar and the noise level was even louder than that in the first room.

Gerry was led to Mary's table. "Hello, Aunt Mary." She kissed the offered cheek.

Mary had an almost empty martini glass in front of her. "Again," she said to the young woman, who signalled the bartender, then asked if Gerry would like a drink. Gerry said she would—a glass of white wine.

"Well," she said brightly, "thank you for inviting me. I've never been here before."

"You have, you know, when you were a baby. Your parents came here with you when they were visiting Maggie. Geoff and

I—" She broke off to take a deep breath. "We invited you as a family. Margaret—" Here Mary took another deep breath and a gulp of her martini. "And Andrew were teenagers. I remember you cried a lot so your mother took you out into the hall and showed you the trophies."

Their drinks arrived. "Fast service," Gerry complimented the waitress.

"Are you ready to order?" the girl, a teenager, asked.

"Wait. Don't I know you?" Gerry asked.

The girl nodded. "I was in your art history class last term."

Gerry remembered that the girl had been utterly bored and she'd had to repeatedly ask her to put away her phone. "Right. Morgan, is it?"

"Yeah. You need more time to make up your minds?"

"I will have the salmon," Mary stated with dignity. "With rice. And a glass of white wine. Gerry?"

Gerry, who'd only had a moment to scan her menu, closed it. "I'll have what you're having, Aunt Mary. Except I already have the wine. And can I have a glass of water, please?" Morgan left their table and Gerry leaned closer to her aunt in order to be heard. "I wish I remembered being here with you and the family. It would have been a nice memory."

"Yes. Well." After Morgan brought Mary's wine and Gerry's water, Mary nodded in the retreating girl's direction. "You're settling in. People already know you."

"I guess. So tell me about the yacht club. Have you belonged to it for long?"

"Well, my grandfather Albert Coneybear was a founding member of the club, in 1909. And my father sailed, of course. Your father seemed to enjoy it. My father had a small yacht but it could sleep eight in a pinch. Geoff didn't sail—golf was his game—but I made him join once we were married. It was a place to come and be social; somewhere for the kids to swim in the summer."

There was a pause. Gerry filled it by remarking, "I've got some renovation going on at the moment."

"Oh yes?"

"We've started by knocking a hole in the dining room wall—behind the downstairs toilet in the alcove I showed you. Remember?" Mary nodded. "And you'll never guess what."

"What?"

"The old family store is still in there. The desk, the pigeonholes for the mail, shelves. Even barrels and boxes—empty, of course. It's like they just said 'Enough' one day and walled it up. Strange, eh?"

Their suppers arrived. Each was a perfectly nice portion of salmon served on a bed of white rice, accompanied by asparagus and a few cherry tomatoes. A yellow sauce on the salmon was bland but buttery.

They tucked in and a silence fell for a few moments. Mary broke it. "I don't remember my father ever mentioning a store in the house. I mean we knew there had been one; he just didn't talk about it."

Gerry swallowed. "I wonder why," she said thoughtfully. "Did it have to do with his brother Alfred? The one who was killed in the war?"

"I have no idea. Do you want dessert? I recommend the chocolate layer cake or the baked Alaska."

"Oo, yes please. Cake, I think." Gerry smiled up at Morgan who was removing their plates. "Are you working here all summer, Morgan?"

"Yeah. Probably. So two chocolate cakes?" They nodded.

"And coffee," Mary called after Morgan's retreating back. "I think she didn't hear me. You haven't finished your wine."

"Lately it doesn't taste very good to me." She added hastily, "Nothing against the wine here. It might be the allergy medication I'm taking. Did your father go to war?"

"No. He was asthmatic. And he only turned eighteen at the end of the war. Not that they wouldn't have taken him at fifteen or sixteen. Alfred was only sixteen, I believe. And Dad's oldest brother, John, had a bad leg, some injury to the knee from skiing, I seem to remember. So he lived to marry Isabelle Parsley, Constance's twin."

Gerry remembered Constance had been Prudence's mother. "Isabelle and John didn't have any children, did they?"

"How do you know that?" Mary said in a surprised voice.

"I've got the family tree. Painted on a big board. It's in the woodshed. I copied it onto paper. I like looking at it. I'm an only child, so I guess I'm interested in families." Their cake and, happily, coffee arrived. "So good," Gerry managed, her mouth full.

"Maggie made that board. Which is funny as she didn't have any children either. She liked history, though." They both paused as the remembrance of the previous year's tragedy sunk in. Mary put down her fork and said in a matter-of-fact voice, "It was a year ago tomorrow, you know."

"I know," Gerry said in a hushed voice. "I'm so sorry."

"No. *I'm* sorry," Mary replied grimly. "So very, very sorry." They finished their dessert in silence.

"Well," said Gerry, draining her coffee. "I must apologize for having to eat and, er, paddle, but I canoed here and I can see the sun is setting. I don't want to be on the water after dark. Not when I'm this far from home."

"You're kidding! You canoed here?" Mary extended her hand and said in a low voice, "I'm glad you came."

Gerry kissed her aunt and left the room. Standing in front of the bathroom mirror, picturing her mother in the room with baby Gerry, she blinked back a few tears, but they were tears of happiness as well as pain. As she got into her canoe she reflected that the evening had gone better than she'd expected.

As she canoed home, she watched as the inhabitants of Lovering settled in for the evening, their lights coming on, some curtains being drawn, others left open, and as she drew near her house and glanced towards Edwina Murray's, she saw one light, shaded, in the author's study, where, presumably, she was hard at work.

15

Now and then comes a clutter of drops against the glass made by a gust of wind. (1841)

"And I looked everywhere, but no sign of any letters from Alfred. I mean, unless he couldn't write or something, there must be letters." Gerry sounded exasperated.

"How late did you stay up last night?" Prudence sipped her coffee.

"Too late," Gerry replied gloomily. "I went through all the family documents again. In the boxes upstairs."

Prudence knew to which boxes she referred. They'd looked through them several times over the last year. She sighed. The day was as gloomy as Gerry's voice had been. "May twenty-seventh," Prudence said sadly.

Gerry couldn't think of anything to say so simply echoed her. "May twenty-seventh." They both stared out the window at the lake, thinking of the woman who should have been with them.

Rain poured off the roof and bounced onto the path. A thick mist covered the lake and they could only see, dimly, the near shore.

Terry and Lucie had phoned to say that they would be working on another project at another house but would return on Friday if the weather was fine. And that the exposed wall was well protected. So much for their ability to predict the weather, Gerry had thought.

Prudence had gotten a lift from one of her neighbours. Gerry had been still asleep when she'd arrived at 8:30, and, probably because of the weather, so had most of the cats.

Prudence had made the coffee, fed the cats and attended to the litter boxes before Gerry, yawning, had trailed down the stairs.

Now they sat where they'd so often sat at the living room table. "I need more coffee," Gerry concluded.

"Good thing I made a big pot," Prudence replied. They sat a little longer in silence listening to the rattle and hiss of the rain before Prudence sighed again and rose. "Better get cracking. Do you have any rhubarb already picked?"

Gerry stretched. "No. Why?"

"You should make pie. I brought a good recipe."

"But I still have leftover coffee cake," Gerry protested.

"You can freeze that. You'll be glad of it sometime when you don't have time to bake."

"All right. I'll go out and get some." Gerry sounded much more cheerful, now that there was the prospect of warm pie in the immediate future. She went upstairs and dressed, then found her raincoat and rubber boots and clumped outside.

She took a deep breath. No more sneezing. Dr. Barron knew what she was doing. She hoped the doctor wasn't too uncomfortable recovering from her injuries. She surveyed the grounds.

The artist in her preferred the grey wet day to a bright sunny one. The greens were saturated with water and popped visually against the bare brown earth, dull sky. Flowers too took on different tints, more delicate. Every object was soft-edged. I'd love to paint this, she thought.

"I'm sorry you had to die, Aunt Maggie," she murmured but then finished her thought silently: that she'd been allowed to come and live at The Maples, that her aunt had left the house to her, made her soberly grateful. Right—rhubarb. She squelched across the lawn.

The rhubarb leaves both repelled and trapped rain drops, depending on each leaf's angle. She released eight stalks, trimmed them, and walked back to the house. The mist on the lake moved, began to break up.

She hung her dripping coat and kicked off her boots in the little porch off the kitchen. Prudence had left a tiny square of paper on the counter. Gerry read: Spicy Rhubarb Pie. "Yum! Spicy!" She set to work.

The recipe was one of those annoying ones that listed "Pastry for a 2-crust pie" as the first ingredient. Once that would have meant instant dismissal of the idea of any pie making for Gerry. But no more. She rummaged in the kitchen drawer where an old food-stained green school folder holding Aunt Maggie's collection of recipes lay under a fairly clean buff file folder for Gerry's own new, albeit slim, collection.

She extracted the recipe for the aptly named "foolproof pastry" and grinned. Of course Prudence would have given her a recipe called that! The pastry had to chill, so after making it she moved on to preparing the pie filling. It couldn't have been easier.

"Mix sugar, rhubarb, tapioca—tapioca!? Oh, Prudence has changed it to flour—that's okay. Mix that with butter, cinnamon, nutmeg, cloves and a pinch of salt." She chopped the rhubarb, and the butter, and dusted them with the dry ingredients, then popped the bowl into the fridge.

She was just finishing cleaning up when Prudence opened the kitchen door a crack, thereby repelling any cats anxious to get to their kibble. "I've had a thought."

"Just one?" Gerry wisecracked. She dried her hands and followed Prudence through the house. "This is very mysterious," she commented. Cats, pleased that the infernal racket of the vacuum cleaner had ceased, began to reappear.

Prudence stopped in the dining room in front of the store. "In there. In the desk. Papers, maybe? Maybe letters?"

"But it's locked," Gerry protested. "And I don't want to break it."

"Wait a minute." Prudence left then returned with a long metal rod. "Meat skewer. Let's see—" She knelt in front of the desk, inserted the skewer and fiddled a bit. There was a "snick" and the desk's lid lifted slightly.

"You are amazing!" said Gerry, rushing to push the lid open.

"I thought it might be like those catches that hold the car hood down," Prudence replied modestly. "My driving instructor made me practise releasing the hood when she showed me all the liquids that have to be checked."

"Good instructor," Gerry absently observed, looking and handling all the papers, some bundled, some loose, that were revealed. "I was never taught that."

"Pie?" Prudence queried.

"The dough chills as we speak," Gerry answered. "And the filling's ready."

"Well, I'll leave you to your desk, then." Prudence could soon be heard above Gerry's head, vacuuming the staircase.

"Too dark," Gerry muttered, and fetched a lamp. In vain did she look for an electrical socket in the store. Once she'd retrieved an extension cord, she settled down on the chair in front of the desk and dug in. Several cats decided they found this new room interesting enough to settle down in and kept her company.

Bob, for one, of course, because when Gerry was stationary he liked to supervise her activities. And Jay, who probably saw Gerry as her second mother after Mother the cat. Besides, there were new corners to be explored, new ledges to be leapt up on to, new hiding places. The boys and Ronald were similarly intrigued and prowled and pounced on each other until the room's novelty wore off and they left in search of different adventures, much to the relief of Gerry, who found their vocalizations distracting.

Bob and Jay dozed. Soon all that could be heard was the vacuum cleaner going further and further away, the rain outside, the ticking of the nearby dining room clock, and the shuffle of old paper, being handled for the first time in almost a century.

PART 4

THE CASE AGAINST
NORMAN CRUMBLES

Melancholy flicked an ear and shifted position slightly so the large downward-tilted leaf was no longer releasing a regular cascade of water drops onto her. She felt Lovey close by, similarly hunched, his fur somewhat damp, but his warmth, from which she drew so much comfort, steady.

Neither of them purred in their semi-conscious state—it was too physically uncomfortable a day—but if they'd been asked, and had deigned to answer, they would have expressed contentment. They were together. Together they both felt better. Melancholy's terrors had lessened since Lovey had joined the pride at The Maples; and the still resonating ache Lovey felt for his lost owner, who'd handled him with care and compassion for seven years before giving him up, was healing. They dozed.

Outside the shelter of the plant, a fine drizzle was falling. The cats were aware of the sound of thousands of droplets striking various surfaces. Of the usual rustlings of bird and rodent, they heard little, though an occasional frog croaked from the lake; the odd toad left its burrow to sit blinking, waiting for some insect morsel to appear.

They sensed Kitten was roaming around, the only other cat of their household who had ventured out in the wet weather. Being an immature, so much their junior in rank, she barely registered.

Melancholy flicked the other ear. Her fur was designed to repel water and it hadn't been raining hard when she and Lovey had dashed from the back of the house to the big plant at the edge of the lawn. Now that they'd been sheltering under its relative dryness for the duration of one catnap, her fur had dried and the ground below her had warmed.

Neither cat could express, or indeed, felt the need to express why they'd made the hurried run through the rain, and any human watching would have thought simply the black one was chasing the tortoiseshell one. They're playing, a person uneducated in the ways of cats might have thought.

Of course, the true interpretation of the scene was that Lovey had followed Melancholy, who was, more than most, attuned to the goings-on at the house. And Melancholy had been prompted, for some reason, to position herself between the lake and the shed. She waited and Lovey waited with her.

The lake appeared to recede into the mist that filled the space between its surface and the sky. The little ripples that lapped the shore could have been going in either direction. Melancholy felt disoriented and centred at the same time.

The mist began to break up as midday approached; bits detached and dissipated. Other bits detached and drifted separately, just as the iced-up lake had broken into separate chunks and floated away to melt. The damp air was unpleasant. Melancholy shivered. Lovey moved closer.

A particular bit of mist detached and drifted over the water toward the rocky shore where the girl's canoe rested. It passed the canoe and continued to the thicket that separated the cats' house and the house where the black dog lived. The thicket was behind the plant where Melancholy and Lovey were hunkered down and both cats swivelled their heads to watch the mist out of the corners of their eyes.

The mist took on the shape of a woman, reduced by age to a small bent form. She paused in the thicket, looking towards the long white house beyond. Then she seemed to become aware of something or someone, for she turned and looked at the cats' house. She moved across the lawn and up the steps leading to the parking pad.

Melancholy made up her mind and sprinted after the ghost (for a ghost, the cat now recognized, it was), coming to pause next to the shed where a small roof overhang gave limited shelter. Lovey, after a moment of frozen surprise, followed.

The ghost approached what the two cats thought of as their ghost, the young woman who waited in her mauve dress at the edge of the road; waited for someone, they felt sure.

But their young woman was oblivious even to the second spirit who came close to her, whispering wetly in her ear as a wind blew off the lake, shaking the trees, who scattered their accumulated raindrops over the scene.

The second spirit observed her friend was not to be distracted. She sighed, and the cats saw her move past their spirit along the road toward the church, as the woman in the mauve dress waited and watched for the one who never came home.

16

All the rest came cluttering about him, crying that
he should haste away to the campe. (1598)

"I made you a ham and cheese and put the pie in the oven," Prudence called from the dining room. "Come and eat your lunch and tell me what you've found."

A tearful, dusty Gerry emerged from the store, holding a packet of letters. "It's all here," she choked. "Just let me wash."

A few minutes later and she was wolfing down her lunch and chattering to Prudence. "So he volunteered right away—Alfred—and he wasn't even fifteen yet! He and some other local boys went together: some Parsleys; Jonas Petherbridge—he was Uncle Geoff's father; a Catford. Alfred's friends and neighbours, I guess. Some of them, including Alfred, lied about their ages. I expect they thought—" She choked up again. "They thought it was all a big adventure." She pushed a collection of letters across the table to Prudence, who began looking at them with a sombre face. The oven timer pinged and Prudence got up to check the pie.

"A few more minutes," she said. "So these are his letters to his family?"

Gerry nodded. "He wrote to his parents and to his sister Mary Anne. In the letters to his parents he tried to keep a cheerful tone. He must have been very close to his sister because he told her more of the truth. What he saw." Gerry shuddered. "It's horrible, Prudence."

"I can imagine," Prudence said grimly.

"As far as I can make out there was this one battle at—Yips? Yipes? It's in one of Aunt Maggie's stories but I can't remember how—?"

Prudence supplied the correct pronunciation. "Ypres."

"Oh. Ypres. Ypres took a couple of months. Lots of steady fighting with lulls in between." She pulled out one letter. "Listen to this. 'When we got to the trench there were about three hundred Germans in front about forty yards away and the stench—' Here's another bit. 'The first two nights we slept on a grave of dead Germans who were so close to the surface the ground moved up and down like dough, and the smell—'"Gerry paused and looked at Prudence. "Why was he telling his sister this awful stuff?"

"He had to tell somebody or go crazy?"

"Yeah. Maybe. He says after April twenty-second when the Germans attacked, they were awake for a week."

"That'll make you crazy, not sleeping."

"They were gassed but the wind blew the gas onto the French Algerian troops to their left, who broke ranks and retreated. I don't know if he's exaggerating but he says eight thousand Canadians held off sixty thousand Germans for twenty-two hours under intense shellfire. He saw Dan Parsley get shot in the head. He saw Billy Catford dead on the ground.

"They were relieved after five days and marched back three miles for breakfast, then another two-day battle. Listen. 'Oh, sis, that food tasted so good and just to be able to eat without being fired upon all the while.' Then they fought again for two days, then retreated through a village where it looked like everyone there had been killed. 'The dead—men, women and children—were piled in ruined houses and burned.' He thanks her for sending him cigarettes. And that's the end of the last letter."

She stopped. Both women were stunned by what they'd read. Prudence spoke first. "I knew it was bad, but didn't know the details. I'll look differently at those old newsreels they play on TV every November." She got up slowly and went into the kitchen. "Pie's done."

"I don't feel much like pie just now," Gerry said sadly.

"You will. You will."

Prudence went to wash cat towels while Gerry continued to sit staring dreamily at the lake. If Mr. Postlethwaite, the minister in Aunt Maggie's story, had been to that war, no wonder he'd lost his focus sometimes. She fetched her illustrations of the story and looked at them with fresh eyes.

Seymour hopped onto her lap, circled and kneaded. He purred as he settled. Gerry stroked him. "Oh, Seymour, you are a love." The cat's purr ceased for a moment, then resumed. Almost, she'd almost got his name right. Lovey, he purred. My name is Lovey.

When Prudence took a break mid-afternoon, the women ate their warm pie. The rain petered out, the mist lifted, but the day remained dull. They talked about books, about Gerry's supper with Mary, about the garden. Gerry copied out the rhubarb pie recipe and put it in her folder. She slyly asked Prudence if she was seeing much of Bertie Smith, and upon seeing her friend flush and smile, said, "Aha! Apparently you are!"

"Actually, I'm taking the train in to Montreal on Saturday to spend the day with him in his shop."

Gerry's mouth dropped open. "Are you auditioning for the part of antique dealer's wife?"

"Don't be silly. It will be interesting for me to see how the shop works. Anyway, he closes at three on Saturdays so we thought we'd take a walk on the mountain. If it doesn't rain. Then have supper somewhere."

"Well, it sounds delightful. Enjoy yourself. That reminds me, Doug and the boys are driving back on Sunday. Only three more days!"

Prudence smiled. "I wonder what's happening with Edwina. Has it been quiet over there?"

Gerry nodded. "No more men arriving in cars as far as I could see, if that's what you mean. You'll be able to see yourself tomorrow when you go." She thought of something and went over to the mantelpiece. "Prudence, did anybody ever lose a wedding ring here?" The room got quiet. "Prudence?" Gerry turned to see Prudence looking pale. "Prudence?"

"May I see it?" she said quietly. She took the plain gold band from Gerry's palm. "Yes. I mean one looks very like the other, I suppose. It's probably mine. Where was it? In the garden? That's where I lost it. Gardening without gloves, for some reason."

Gerry shook her head. "No. It was in the pool. A huge crows' nest fell in. When I cleaned up the mess I found the ring. I think the crows had been collecting shiny objects."

"Really? I lost it so long ago." There was an awkward pause.

Prudence closed her hand over the ring and stood. "I'll ask Bertie to sell it for me. Now, I'll finish up here and we can be off."

Gerry drove Prudence home but felt restless. She drove to a nearby town that had a BBQ chicken restaurant, got takeout and drove back to Lovering as the delectable scent filled her car. Dutifully, she fed the cats first, then devoured the meal. I'm so hungry lately, she thought, dipping french fries into sauce. Must be spring.

She went to bed and finished *Purple Angel*. Hah, she thought as she closed the book and rearranged herself among her four feline bedmates. The girlfriend did it.

17

Thumping, shuffling, and cluttering. (1577)

"Aagh! I'm going crazy!" Gerry covered her ears with her hands and retreated inside.

Terry and Lucie had arrived early that morning with a crew—well, with two young men they proudly introduced as their sons, Leonard and Bruce, college students fresh from exams. Lenny was thin like his dad but taller, while Bru was short like Lucie.

All four of them moved the scaffolding from the side to the back of the house, cranked up a radio to a local rock station, and began calling to each other and singing snatches of tunes.

At first Gerry thought it was fine: the family's way of creating a high energy workplace. But as the morning wore on and she tried first gardening—she sadly observed the second catnip plant gnawed down to its roots, dug up and left for dead—then reading inside, she realized she had to get out.

After asking Terry to order a window for the store, soon to be nook, as well as arrange for electricity, she packed a lunch, got into her canoe and paddled away from Lovering, south.

Right away she felt better. Two weeks of vacation were drawing to a close and she wanted to enjoy what was left, in case she decided to resume working the next Monday. She took a deep breath. She reflected that marking the one-year anniversary of Maggie's death had resolved the guilt she felt at inheriting her aunt's property. Aunt Maggie was gone. Gerry was here, alive. She laughed aloud and passed the Parsley Inn.

On its lawn, where gaily painted Adirondack chairs waited for relaxing customers, a diminutive black form tensed, then sprang, then sat back foolishly, paws empty. "Hello, Gregory!" Gerry called and waved. The cat, who could have been Jay only without the white feet and dickie, looked up and mewed, as if saying, "Come and help me hunt."

"You're on your own," Gerry assured him.

"You're on your own," she repeated as she passed the ferry landing and observed the cars lined up waiting. But that's a good thing, she concluded, having noticed thus far in her short life that thinking was difficult when others were present. Past the ferry she entered new territory.

Here was some of the historically agricultural land of Lovering. Historical, because few of the farms remained. A few herds of dairy or beef cattle were left.

Coming to a small cove that abutted the river road, and across from which was one of those farms, and mindful that going back she'd be battling the river's current, she called it quits and beached the canoe. Maybe when Doug was back, they could go farther, around the next point to a huge bay where, from the car, she'd seen herons and other waterfowl congregate in abundance.

Meanwhile, there was a log to sit on and a nice lunch to eat in this peaceful spot where overhanging trees shaded her and birds chirped their hellos and goodbyes. And there was the view.

Across the river, the church at the centre of the village drew the eye, its spire piercing a miniscule part of the endless blue sky.

Gerry got her sketchpad and a pencil from her knapsack and disappeared into sketching. When she was happy with her efforts in that direction she turned around and sketched the approach to the farm—its long dirt driveway, leaning fence posts on either side; grass for hay growing in one field; and away in the distance, in a field closely cropped and decorated with cow plops, the herd, munching.

After a while, she sighed, put away her drawings, and rummaged in her knapsack for the orange marzipan cat she'd found in the back of her fridge. That trip across the lake with Bea ten days ago seemed like it had happened months earlier.

She nibbled at the cat, beginning at its tail. It seemed mean to just bite off its head. When she'd finished that, she thought she'd like to walk for a bit.

Next to the farm's driveway she could see an agricultural road in even worse repair, gravelled, deeply rutted. She hoisted her knapsack and crossed the main road. I wouldn't take the Mini up here, she thought, dodging potholes filled with rainwater. It could fall in and drown!

Trees arched over the road, making a pale green cover. Red-winged black birds and field sparrows called and fluttered. The walk was lovely but uninteresting. Her mind wandered.

There were a number of choices for murderer of Roald Henderson. She lined them up in her mind. Edwina, Andrea, debt collectors. None of them seemed quite right. So. Someone else, still in the shadows. A random act of violence? If Roald's gun was the one that killed him, not random, otherwise why try to implicate Edwina by leaving the gun at her house? Unless that had been an accident, the gun dropped when the car with Roald's body in it had been either driven away or, empty, returned. And Gerry was pretty sure the police wouldn't believe Edwina's story about the blood in her trunk being squirrel's. Or only squirrel's.

Trying to suggest that Roald's death was the result of random violence was dubious because everyone knew that the spouse was the number one suspect. But if it was deliberate violence, who stood to gain from Roald's death? Only Edwina, unfortunately, Gerry's mind reasoned. And who stood to gain from Edwina going to prison? It wasn't like she would lose her money or her house as a result. Did she have some distant relative who needed money? It didn't make sense either way.

This seemed too complicated to Gerry. She reached the train tracks, saw that the road continued along in the same straight fashion on the other side and turned around. She heard the signal for a train approaching and turned back to look.

Gordon Conway passed her in his short train—four passenger cars and the sleek engine—and took in Gerry's hopping and waving form. He looked astonished but as he passed gave her a quick rendition of "Shave and a haircut, two bits" on the train's horn. Toot, tooty toot toot—toot, toot.

She was delighted. Then her previous thoughts returned, as she remembered Gordon had discovered Roald's body on the tracks. She hoped he hadn't been traumatized. Random violence seemed the most obvious solution. Except for the gun. Why leave it under the car? She realized she was going in circles, logic-wise, and gave it up.

"Time to check in on the workers," she said, and quickened her pace.

By the time she got home, she was sweaty. All she wanted was a shower but was brought to a pause on the lawn when she saw Terry and Lenny were working on the window space for the nook. "Did you already get the window?" she asked incredulously.

"It's a standard size so I sent Bru to get it," Terry replied. They'd unblocked the window space and were measuring and fitting shims around the square opening. Gerry went to see from inside.

Now that the nook was lit by natural light, she could see what it might have been like to work there. It would have been brightest in the morning, and in winter when the sun shone low and briefly through the eastern aperture. She could picture the family— perhaps the father, the sons, or, as June's diorama suggested, the daughter, Mary Anne, serving behind the counter.

And she could even see a little further back to a time when the post and provisions arrived via the river; see men walking up the lawn carrying the same; saw the orientation of the house shift from facing the road, to facing the river. For the first time she wondered about the Mohawk who lived across the river, what their part in all this trade could have been. I bet they weren't afraid to cross the river in their canoes, she thought. Or paddle at night.

She shook herself, realizing Terry was speaking from outside the window. "Bru's back. Come have a look before we fit it." She went outside. The window was a simple square, stained medium-brown and with a crank. "Couldn't have found a vintage window quickly. You can always put one in later. And I didn't think you'd want a white plastic one. The dark wood will match the interior and we'll paint the outside frame white to match the other windows. Okay?"

"Very okay." She heard the phone ring. "Excuse me." She ran indoors.

"Gerry? It's me, Judith. I think I found what you're looking for. May I come to see the store?"

"Sure, Judy. When do you want to come?"

"Is now okay? Tomorrow I'm covering a few events and I'd like to write the piece about the store tonight."

"Sure. See you soon."

Gerry made a pot of tea and set out the rest of the pie. It wasn't long before she was showing Judy the store. Judy had brought her camera and took several pictures.

"It's good you're photographing it now, because I'm going to rearrange it into a reading nook."

"I'll give you copies of these. Dad liked my idea for an article. Something like 'Mystery Room Uncovered at The Maples.'"

They had their tea in the dining room so they could look at the store. From outside, the workers could be heard.

"I'll also put in that you're renovating this beautiful example of early Lovering history, etc. Now, here's what I found. Well, not that I found much. But I noticed, when I went back to the 1890s and early 1900s, there were small ads for The Maples store as a place where people could get supplies delivered and which offered—let me see—" She found a notebook in her bag. "Um, okay, offered 'A Selection of Staple and Luxury Products.' And then, after 1915, nothing."

"I guess we'll never know," Gerry said slowly. "But maybe after two of their children died, the Coneybears couldn't face the public, couldn't keep going. And then during the war, they must not have been able to get many of the products they provided anyway, so the store just fizzled out."

"And someone else took over," Judy said triumphantly. "Look. Remember the Goodman family store? By the 1920s they were operating a post office and shop out of their house just before you get to the Parsley Inn. It's quite interesting. There was a gas station and candy and ice cream store nearby, and a library. It was a miniature village."

"Yes. My aunt wrote a little story about going by bicycle to the candy store, much later of course, with her brother and sister."

"This pie is great!" Judy scraped her plate.

"Have another piece," Gerry offered. "It's not like I'm going to run out of rhubarb." They finished the pie and Judy left. Gerry gave the cats their supper.

The workers had left and she wandered over to the store. Lightning and Seymour followed her. The new window was in place. She cranked it open and closed a few times, then tried to remove some of the wooden casks and boxes from the room, to make more space. But she found she couldn't do it. Let it be a store for a little longer, she thought. From the new opening in the wall, the two cats watched her.

18

I heard such a clutter of small shot—"Murder! murder! murder!" (1702)

It had been a lovely day, and Gerry still felt a bit sticky after her extensive canoeing. She changed into a green bikini and her short red Japanese kimono, grabbed a towel and sauntered down to the pool.

Those cats that had finished dining began to appear in the garden and a few likewise sauntered down to investigate her. She dipped her toe in the water. "Brrr! No way I'm creeping down the ladder inch by inch, cats. I'll chicken out."

The cats—Bob, Jay, the boys, Ronald and Mother—perked up at the mention of chicken but, realizing she didn't have any, resumed circling the pool, watching the tiny ripples and play of sunlight through leaves on its surface. Gerry plunged in, feet first, and came up gasping.

"No, really," she spluttered, "it's fine," and splashed water near her little gang. The gang withdrew, looking offended. First, no chicken, and now purposefully aiming water at them. She laughed and did a few laps.

When she paused to tread water, she was surprised to see Edwina Murray hovering poolside.

"Edwina, how are you? Is something wrong?"

"Can we talk? I'm stuck."

Not understanding exactly what she meant by that remark, Gerry ushered her guest back to the house. She changed and wound a fresh towel around her hair before making coffee. The swim had energized her and she felt great.

Edwina, meanwhile, had been walking up and down on the stone path behind the house. Gerry called her to the screened back porch. "Better have our coffee in here. The mosquitoes are starting."

"Are they? I hadn't noticed."

Gerry offered the coffee and remarked with a nervous laugh, "We always seem to catch each other with wet hair."

Edwina sipped her coffee and stared gloomily at the lake.

"What did you mean by being 'stuck,' Edwina?"

"It's the case. I'm three quarters through and I can't decide. Is he guilty or not? Will she or won't she?"

Gerry frowned. How did Edwina know the case was seventy-five percent finished? "Have the police gotten back to you about the blood? Or the gun?"

"Eh?" Edwina looked disoriented. "Oh. That. Yes, I suppose. The blood in the trunk is Roald's. And his gun was used to kill him. Yes. No. I mean. How do I decide if he has to die? Or is it all a huge mistake?"

It was Gerry's turn to look bewildered. "I'm not sure—" she began.

"Let me start at the beginning," Edwina said.

"I think you better!"

"So. Norman owes a lot of money. He's selfish, thinks the world owes him. He also cheats on his wife, so she plans to murder him. Are you with me so far?"

"Yes," Gerry said faintly, feeling no less confused but willing to wait for clarification.

"So. The wife is the narrator, and all through the first three sections she tries to get up the courage to kill Norman. She tries to justify the killing to herself, and to the reader. This is supposed to build tension, as the reader never knows when she's going to do it. Or if.

"For example: there's a scene where she's slicing meat with a big knife and he comes up close to her and tries to, tries to kiss her." Here Edwina's eyes glittered. "And you wonder, is this it? Is she going to do it now? Or in another scene, say, they're—"

"I think I grasp the technique," Gerry said quickly, feeling a bit disturbed. "Don't give too much away."

"Oh. Right. Well. Now I've built up all that tension, I'm not sure I *want* her to be the murderer. Or even for him to be murdered. Do you see?"

"I think so. We're talking about the plot of your next book."

"Yes. What else?"

"Oh. Um. I thought maybe about Roald's death."

Edwina waved her hand impatiently. "The police will look after all that. I have to finish this book. I have a two-book-a-year deal and the deadline for this one is in a few weeks. Then I have to start the next one. So I'm under a lot of pressure."

Gerry tried to concentrate on the hypothetical murder. "Okay. So is, er, Norman definitely going to be murdered?"

"Well, that's just it. The book's title is *The Case Against Norman Crumbles*. So the double entendre lends itself to several interpretations."

"Wait." Gerry held up a hand. "Is his full name Norman Crumbles?" When Edwina nodded, Gerry said, "Oh, now I get it. The would-be murderer is trying to build up a case for murdering him but the title indicates she may not do it. But then someone else does or does not. Quite a quandary." She paused. "Don't you think, Edwina, that seeing as your husband has just been murdered, it's maybe not, er, appropriate to publish this book at this time?"

Edwina looked at her and spoke calmly. "Let me explain a few things to you. One, it won't be published for another year.

Two, the publicity surrounding Roald's death will be good for the book. Three, as I didn't kill Roald, it's fine. It's going to be fine." She nervously fiddled with her teaspoon. "Besides, I can't change it now. I have to keep going. I've written two versions. I just have to decide."

"Well, you know best," Gerry said doubtfully. "About publishing, I mean." She threw a sideways glance at Edwina. "Did the police have anything to say when they told you about the gun and blood?"

"Just that I was a person of interest and not to try to leave the vicinity," Edwina said absently. "I told them I had a book to finish and couldn't go away even if I wanted to."

Gerry wondered what the police had made of such a response. Edwina certainly came across as an innocent. Indiscreet, but an innocent. "Oh, here's Prudence," she said, observing that woman cutting through the thicket coming from Edwina's.

"I should go," Edwina said, standing.

"Do you feel clearer about the book?" Gerry asked.

"Not really." Edwina suddenly smiled. "But thank you for listening. I'll sleep on it. Maybe take a day off. The deadline will just have to wait." She nodded at Prudence as the two passed each other.

"What's up?" Gerry queried.

Prudence looked worriedly over her shoulder. "It's Edwina. I heard her on the phone, talking and laughing with somebody. She sounded quite joyful."

"Well, what's wrong with that?" Gerry replied. "Maybe it was a good friend she was talking to."

Prudence looked uncertain. "Maybe. But she said quite clearly, 'He had to die and he's dead. And I for one am glad.' Then she *laughed*."

Now Gerry looked doubtful. "Well I just had a fairly confusing talk with her. *She* was talking about her book and *I* thought she was talking about Roald. We sorted it out in the end. I think. But she said she hadn't yet made up her mind about whether to kill the husband in the book or not. Not like what you heard during the phone call. But she did say she'd written two versions."

"I may have misheard. But it makes me uneasy hearing her. As does that dog. It just sits there and stares."

"Oh, Shadow's all right. It's just his grave character. He's grieving too, remember?"

"Well, Edwina certainly isn't."

"No, she isn't, is she?" Gerry removed her towel from her head and shook her mostly dry hair loose. "I just remembered something. From our tea party last week. Edwina said she'd been in Montreal all the previous day. But when I took the ferry that morning I saw a man and woman who I assumed were her and Roald arguing in the backyard. Then the guy drove away in a yellow car and the woman went inside the house. There was also a red car parked there. I did see them from a long way away," she added doubtfully.

Prudence spoke slowly. "Edwina and Roald's cars are both black, aren't they? So either Edwina is lying or somebody else was at her house with Roald that day. But who? The girlfriend?"

"Andrea drives a red car, as far as I know. Maybe she has another one that's yellow. But how do we know the man was Roald? Would he be likely to leave her alone in his and Edwina's house?" Gerry sounded puzzled and added, "It's so sleazy to think he'd have his girlfriend over to his wife's house. I mean, really?"

"But that's just it—he was a sleazy guy. And maybe he just drove off to get something and she was waiting for him. If Edwina took the train or had an appointment, they'd know roughly when to expect her back."

"I guess." Gerry changed the subject. "Looking forward to your date tomorrow?"

Prudence smiled a little. "Yes. I am."

19

The coaches, horsemen and crowd, cluttered away,
to be out of harm's way. (1724)

That evening Gerry cleared her head of murder—both fictional and real—by beginning another Swallows and Amazons book—*Winter Holiday*. In many ways it was one of the most beguiling in the series she'd read thus far. The children from three different families enjoyed their school Christmas vacation at the same location as their summer ones—a village on one of England's Lake District's largest lakes—skating and sledding to their hearts' content. Then, on the last day of the holidays, one of them got mumps, which meant all the rest were in quarantine for at least another month. No school!

She settled in to read about their subsequent adventures and was surprised when she yawned and realized the sun had set and the back porch was no longer a comfortable temperature. She went up to bed, wondering how the next day was going to unfold.

Up early, she packed a box of books—*The Cake-Jumping Cats of Dibble*—as backup, prepared a coffee in a travel mug and drove to a nearby bookstore. As she drove, she hoped Terry and Lucie would show up to work while she was away. She was impatient to get the house finished.

The bookstore was devoted to children's literature. This would be Gerry's first experience trying to sell her book in any bookstore. She felt a bit nervous. She didn't have any particular way with kids. What if they didn't like her? Or the book?

The bookstore owner was a thin, worried-looking woman. She ushered Gerry into the small shop and showed her the display of her book. Gerry's heart sank. There must be twenty copies of her book piled there. She thought of how hard it had been to sell even four or five copies when she'd sat with CRASpo volunteers for the whole day in local malls. She'd never sell twenty books in the two hours the owner had allotted her. And then the woman wouldn't ever want to host Gerry again.

For the first hour, things looked bleak. Gerry sat at a little table and tried to attract kids and parents to her book. She sold two.

Then at a little before eleven, more parents with kids in tow entered and the store owner unrolled a shaggy carpet for the kids to sit on. She turned to Gerry. "All right. You're on."

"On?" an aghast Gerry replied.

"On. Your reading. I advertised. Go ahead." She turned her head aside and whispered. "Take your time. Point to the pictures. Haven't you done this before?"

Gerry nodded numbly (though she hadn't), took a copy of her book and dragged her chair over in front of the kids. The owner introduced her, everybody clapped and Gerry began.

Once she started, the essential silliness of cats training for a competition in which they jumped over elaborate confections set up on tables—with subsequent disasters and everyone in the book enjoying a variety of desserts at every turn—she quite enjoyed herself, inventing different voices for the different characters: a buoyant optimistic one for Max Scarfnhatznmitz; a humble one for Lady Tess Ponscomb; a haughty one for Queen Atholfass of Fasswassenbasset. And when she enjoyed herself, so did the kids.

They drooled when she described the cakes and laughed when the feline and canine characters did foolish things. At the end of the reading, the applause was much louder than it had been at the beginning and they sold out the books in the shop. She had to run out to the car to get the extra copies she'd brought from home.

The owner was pleased, told her to come again, and said she'd order more books to repay Gerry for any of her own copies they'd sold, as well as to stock the store. It was an exhausted but triumphant Gerry who drove home for lunch thinking of a sequel.

By the look of it, her work crew had been and gone. Fair enough. A half day on Saturday. They'd finished the back of the house and moved the scaffolding to the front, ready to start there on Monday.

She found a note under a stone on the step at the side door. "Ordered more insulation. May arrive today. Terry." He'd put a smiley face next to his name.

A ham and cheese on a croissant with lashings of mayo and hot mustard would hit the spot. She took it and a big glass of milk onto the back porch and settled down with *Winter Holiday*. Before she sank into her book, she gave a thought to the cats. Many if not most could be seen in the backyard and garden.

Fluffy Blackie and her brother, equally fluffy Whitey (who should really have been called Beigey, but never mind) were playing tag over near some tall purple flowers Gerry didn't recognize.

Bob slunk across the lawn, pausing to freeze with one paw lifted, so much like a retriever that Gerry almost laughed out loud. He vanished under the gate that separated her and Blaise's property. Good thing Bob's arch-enemy Graymalkin was away staying with Blaise's Montreal relations or there might have been trouble.

Gerry could see Cocoon, an elderly grey and white, a quiet lady, dozing under the hydrangea that had been Marigold the cat's command post when she still lived. The kitten Jay flitted by, chasing a small orange butterfly, paused, and looked at Cocoon. You could see Jay's little brain assess: would it be more fun to disturb the old cat or continue with the butterfly? The butterfly fluttered and that decision was made. Jay was off.

Kitty-Cat and Harley stalked by on the stone path near the house. They really do look like cows, Gerry thought, finishing her sandwich. "Moo," she said, toasting them with her milk. Funny, she thought, that I haven't had a taste for wine lately.

The boys and Ronald streaked through the perennial garden down toward Yalta. Maybe I'll swim later, she thought, and stretched.

On her fingers she counted the number of cats she'd seen: eleven. She guessed Lightning and Seymour were probably in their new favourite spot by the shed, so that made thirteen.

Just then she caught sight of Jinx, a grey longhair with a white bib, skirting the left edge of the lawn where the rhubarb was, intent on a bird that was hopping from stone to stone by the shore. Max, an orange and white longhair, was approaching the same bird from the right.

Are they working as a team, she wondered? Evidently not, as Max caught sight of Jinx and froze. Jinx also saw Max and froze. The bird flew away. Both cats took refuge from embarrassment by sitting down and grooming, then walking away from each other. Doot dee doo, Gerry thought. The social niceties of the cat world.

She'd lost count of her cats, but figured the rest must be in the house. She opened her book.

She got to the part where Dick and Dot had mistaken a signal from the other kids for their cue to leave on a dash to an imaginary North Pole. As it was evening and a snowstorm was threatening, it promised to be an exciting adventure.

She was distracted by the sound of raised voices coming from Edwina's backyard. She closed her book and leaned forward. The voices sounded angry.

She couldn't see, so she left the porch and walked down the stone steps to the lawn, pausing on the last step. The voices were getting louder. Two women. She recognized Edwina's and could guess who owned the other. Andrea. Cats, also distracted from their activities, were listening and looking.

"I don't like this," murmured Gerry. She was beginning to make out parts of what the women were saying.

Edwina: "Blah no way blah first blah blah got blah kidding me, you blah."

Andrea: "Blah blah so blah never thought blah blah mean, just mean!"

Gerry walked out into the middle of the lawn and surveyed the scene.

The two women were facing each other on the driveway outside Edwina's back door. Edwina was hunched and her arms were crossed defensively over her chest. The shorter Andrea gesticulated wildly with her hands as she spoke and paced back and forth in front of Edwina, who flinched every time the other came near.

With a final, "I know you did it! I know!" from Andrea, which Gerry clearly heard, Andrea stomped to her car parked behind Edwina's, reached in to its open window and turned, brandishing a gun.

"No!" yelled Gerry and began to run towards the two women. Edwina froze. Andrea half-turned and the gun went off. Glass tinkled. Gerry dove into the thicket. Cats, among them Mother and Runt, who must have been busy in there, shot out of the underbrush. Only old fat Min Min, who was deaf, remained to calmly walk over and greet Gerry, who was face down in the violets. She heard his friendly purr and wet nose on her cheek.

"You broke my window! You damaged my property!" Gerry heard Edwina shriek. She raised her head.

Andrea must have dropped the gun, or perhaps Edwina, made brave defending her beloved house, had wrestled it from her, because now Edwina was pointing it at Andrea. "Get off my property!" Edwina thundered. Andrea tore back to the red convertible, which she speedily reversed out Edwina's circular driveway, taking a portion of the low white picket fence with her.

"Edwina!" Gerry yelled. "Put the gun down!"

Edwina looked around wildly to see where the voice was coming from.

"It's me, Gerry. I'm in the thicket. It's okay. She's gone."

"It's not okay!" Edwina yelled back as she lowered the gun. "My window's shattered! Do you know how much those windows cost? They're custom!"

"I'm coming over there, all right?" Gerry slowly rose and looked over her shoulder at her own property. The beep-beep-beep of a reversing truck told her that the insulation was being delivered. There was not a single cat in sight, except for Min Min, curling around her legs. She looked back at Edwina who was placing the gun on a birch stump outside her door. Now that the humans had ceased their noise, from Edwina's house came the sound of Shadow's frenzied barking.

20

This messenger cluttereth out all at once. (1654)

"Do you want to call the police?" Gerry panted.

"That's the last thing I want to do!" snapped Edwina. "See *them* again!?"

"All right. Go inside," Gerry instructed, "and make some tea. And give me a plastic bag." Edwina handed Gerry a bag from a cache she had in a plant pot near the back door.

"For Shadow," Edwina explained, retreating inside.

Gerry picked up the gun the way she would dog poop—with her hand inside the bag so she didn't touch the gun. After a moment's thought, she ran back to her house, put the gun into her potting shed behind a sack of sheep manure, signed for the delivery of insulation and ran back to Edwina's.

She paused at the back door. She heard the building supplies store's truck leave. She heard that Shadow had stopped barking. What she hoped not to hear was a police siren. All the near neighbours—Blaise, Andrew—were away, and Cathy, she hoped, was busy with weekend customers. There were no houses on the far side of Edwina's, just a small wood. A gun going off in the vicinity was not unknown in the country. Her Uncle Geoff had hunted partridge in the nearby woods. Nobody would call the police, would they? She let herself in.

Shadow came running, a low growl issuing from behind bared teeth, the hackles on his back risen. Gerry froze. "Edwina?" she called in what she hoped was a voice loud enough to be heard but calm enough not to further inflame the dog.

Edwina stuck her head into the hallway. "Shadow! Enough!" The dog padded over to her, his head drooping. She patted him. "Good dog, good dog. Come through, Gerry." Gerry followed them into the kitchen.

Edwina seemed now to be taking it all in stride. Gerry, finding herself suddenly weak at the knees, sat down at the table. "Could I get a drink of water? I feel a bit trembly."

Edwina brought it. "You do look pale. I've put the kettle on. Good thing for me you were outside."

"Yes," Gerry said faintly. "Good thing. What on earth was going on?"

"If you heard any of it, you heard her accuse me of Roald's murder. I accused her back, though, now I reflect, why would she have? Unless he pissed her off the way he used to piss *me* off."

Hearing the normally prim Edwina use such language made Gerry suddenly want to giggle. She repressed the urge, contenting herself with saying, "Well, if he borrowed money from her? And didn't pay her back? That would be infuriating. Or maybe he cheated on her."

Edwina laughed bitterly. "He probably did both. But that's no reason to kill him." She suddenly reddened, realizing what she'd just said. She spoke slowly. "So I guess Andrea and I are or were in the same boat. Poor her."

"But why on earth would she have a gun? And why wave it at you? She must be demented."

"That would be one excuse," Edwina said grimly. She made tea and produced Gerry's rhubarb cake. "Thank you for the cake, by the way. I seem to be becoming more and more in debt to you."

"Oh, go on," Gerry said self-deprecatingly. "Maybe if I hadn't yelled just now, the gun wouldn't have gone off. Maybe Andrea was just using it to scare you."

"It worked. She scared me. But scare me into confessing, you mean?" When Gerry nodded, Edwina said, "Well, that's not going to happen. I'm more and more glad I have Shadow here with me." The dog, lying on the floor near Edwina's feet and hearing his name, lifted his head off his paws and thumped his tail. "I don't think I'll leave the house without him for a while."

"Look at that," Gerry said. "He's warming to you."

"Where did you put the gun?" Edwina asked.

Gerry told her; they agreed to leave it where it was, then chatted a little about writing. When there didn't seem to be anything left to say, Gerry left.

She gave the cats their suppers early and went to bed, pulling the covers over her head. Her nap lasted until the evening; she'd slept deeply but still felt tired. She made a quick snack—some soup with cheese and crackers—and went back to bed, where she finished her book.

Sunday morning she woke up early, still a bit shaky. She made some scrambled eggs with toast and tea and phoned Prudence. "Would you like to go to church with me, Prue? I want to read the First World War plaque again. And I have lots to tell you about Edwina."

There was a pause at the other end. "Are you going to ask how my day with Bertie went?"

"Only if you want to talk about it," Gerry replied in her best "Miss Innocent" voice. "We could go out for lunch if you like. My treat. Let's go to the Parsley."

"All right. Thanks. Sounds nice. I'll meet you at the church."

Feeling better now she'd eaten, and looking forward to having a good gab with Prudence, Gerry showered and put on some church-appropriate clothes—a calf-length full brown skirt with a gold long-sleeved blouse, a floppy cloth hat and sandals—and walked the short distance to St. Anne's.

The little church, up a small rise in the road, always gave her a half-happy, half-sad feeling. She didn't go often but usually left feeling better than she had before. Does that mean I'm feeling bad? she wondered. The previous day had been exhilarating—at the bookstore—and terrifying—at Edwina's. It would be good to step away from those extremes for an hour or so.

She walked through the gate, past the minister's car parked in the short driveway, and along the pink stone path set in the lawn. The church was made from the same stone, as were the gateposts and the low stone wall that separated the small graveyard from Lovering's main road, alongside which a dozen or so cars were parked.

The bell started ringing as she entered. She nodded at the elderly bell-ringer, then chose a pew from which she could read the plaque. Prudence slipped in next to her and they smiled at each other.

After the service, Gerry copied down the list of names from the plaque. I'll put this with his letters, she thought. Then future generations will understand what happened to poor Alfred.

They walked into the graveyard. Gerry found one of her family's monuments—the largest. It had been erected by the family's founder, John Coneybear, 1810–1893, whose name appeared in large letters on the side of the stone facing into the graveyard. There, below his name, was that of his daughter Margaret, 1855–1945, and his son Albert, 1865–1921. (John's wife Sybil and their many children who died in infancy were not afforded a spot on this stone, but that's another story.) One had to move to the left side of the stone to read the names of Margaret's family and to the right to read those of Albert's.

Above Albert's name was engraved BLESSED ARE THE PURE IN
HEART, FOR THEY SHALL SEE GOD. MATTHEW 5:8. Then followed
the names of his wife, Elizabeth Parsley, and their four children,
including Mary Anne and Alfred, both dead by 1915.

On the back of the stone were the details of Albert and
Elizabeth's youngest son, Matthew Coneybear, 1900–1968, and
his wife Ellie Catford, 1914–1970, Gerry's grandparents. And
freshly chiselled into the rock was Aunt Maggie's name: Margaret
Coneybear, 1948–2003. There was nothing to say. That Gerry's
father had chosen for first his wife's and then his own memorials
to be on the stone wall at the rear of the graveyard said something
about his relationship with his parents, Gerry thought. But what,
she wasn't sure.

She and Prudence walked to the memorial wall and paused
before the small brass plaques there. As usual, Gerry touched each
of her parents' plaques briefly.

"Where's your mother buried, Prue?" she asked.

"She isn't. Her urn is in my kitchen," was the somewhat
startling reply. "But here's her plaque, next to her sister's."

Gerry read: Mary Isabelle and Constance Virginia. "Kind of
fancy names," she commented. They walked slowly away.

"Mother told me when they were little they called each
other by their middle names, their secret twin names, they said.
As adults they would sometimes use them when they were being
affectionate or teasing each other. And eventually Mary Isabelle
dropped the Mary and became just Isabelle to everybody."

Prudence wheeled her bike to Gerry's and they drove to the
Parsley Inn. They were shown to a table under an umbrella on
the large lakeside stone patio by one of the four Parsley children,
while another came to take their orders.

Gerry enquired after Gregory, the inn's cat, before ordering
a hamburger with mushrooms and Swiss cheese, while Prudence

chose the salmon. "That's what Mary and I ate at the yacht club last week," Gerry commented.

The blue sky displayed big puffy white clouds. Little boats sported on the blue-grey water. The ferry putted back and forth, and the church spire across the lake gleamed silver.

"Wow!" Gerry exclaimed. "Spectacular. So. How was yesterday?"

"Fine." Their food arrived.

"Just fine?" Gerry shovelled french fries into her mouth.

Prudence ate her lunch in a slow, methodical fashion, frequently putting down knife and fork. "Bertie explained his mark-up formula. It was very interesting."

"And? What's it like upstairs? Where he lives?"

Prudence's cheeks began a slow flush. "We didn't go upstairs, Gerry. We went for a walk. On the mountain. We ate at a Lebanese restaurant. Very good, too. Then I took the late train home."

"Oh." Gerry was aware she sounded disappointed. "Well. He's a nice man. I think," she added uncertainly.

"Yes. I like him."

"So…did you make a plan to get together again?"

"We did." Prudence laid her cutlery across her empty plate.

"And? Geez, Prudence, it's like pulling teeth!"

Prudence smiled up at their waitress. "No dessert for me, thanks."

Gerry burped and covered her mouth. "I'm so sorry! Just the bill, please." The waitress left and she hissed at Prudence, "You're not going to tell me, are you?"

Prudence smiled and stared at the lake.

Gerry lowered her voice. "How do you feel about coming back to my place? I don't feel like discussing Edwina's husband's messy end out here in public."

Prudence nodded and they made their way back to Gerry's. She had just brought a tea tray out to Prudence on the back porch when the phone rang. "Rats!" she said.

"Hello?"

"G-Gerry?" The voice that sobbed at her was so high-pitched Gerry was unsure as to the caller's identity.

"David?" she guessed. David, Doug's youngest son. "What's wrong?" She put a hand over her suddenly nauseous stomach.

"D-Dad. And James. In the h-hospital."

"In the hospital?" Gerry heard her own voice sounding incredulous. "David, what happened?"

"We were driving home." David paused to take a gulp of air and his voice lowered a bit. "Dad wanted to leave this morning so we could be home not too late. James wanted to stay till the afternoon. Go for one more canoe ride. They had an argument but Dad insisted."

He wanted to see me, Gerry thought, so he rushed them. She interrupted David. "David, what happened? Why are they in the hospital?"

"Dad let James drive, to make up for not getting his way. He was going a bit fast. A big moose came out of nowhere. James must have swerved because Dad's side of the car, Dad's side—"

"David, where are you?" He named the hospital, a trauma centre in Ottawa. Gerry's stomach turned. "Are you and Geoff and James all right?"

"Yeah," he said shakily. "More or less. James has a broken arm, maybe his collarbone too. He's gone to x-ray. Geoff is here with me. But, Gerry, Dad's in surgery."

Gerry's stomach lurched. She swallowed the sudden taste of bile in her mouth. She thought quickly. David had called her because the boys' Uncle Andrew was away and their grandmother, Mary, was recovering from her own injury. "Okay. Okay,

David. Did you phone anybody else? No? Okay. I'll phone your grandmother and then I'll drive to you. Okay? Okay. See you in a couple of hours. And David? I love you. It'll be all right."

Oh, God, oh, God, she thought. Will it? Be all right? Then she ran to the toilet and threw up.

PART 5

WILD BLOOD

M elancholy had had a bad day. From the moment she woke and followed the girl downstairs for breakfast, she'd had a feeling of foreboding. Her fur was slightly raised and her tail stump twitched. She snarled at Lovey when he tried to get close and watched him beat a dignified retreat.

All day, as the girl left and returned with the cleaning woman, Melancholy had watched the young woman standing at the end of the driveway, her long mauve skirt fluttering, one hand restlessly clutching the other, looking up and down the road. She appeared to be thinning, becoming even more translucent.

When the girl drove away again, alone, near cat suppertime, and clutching a sack, her face tear-stained, the cleaner waving goodbye with a worried face, Melancholy was not surprised.

She was surprised when the cleaner, after feeding the cats, didn't get on her bicycle and ride away. Instead, she talked on the phone a couple of times in a low serious voice, made supper, watched TV, then went upstairs and fell asleep on top of the girl's bed.

All of the cats were surprised at that. The four who slept with the girl tried to find their usual spots on the bed, but with the cleaner there their patterns were confused. When Top Cat and Lovey got into a hissy fight on top of the bed and the cleaner expressed her displeasure, Melancholy left the room.

It wasn't just the sense of foreboding that was bothering her. She felt her whole disposition was changing. Not that she didn't still feel melancholy from time to time, but it seemed that as long as Lovey's comforting presence was nearby she felt, almost, normal. And as her character was modifying, so was her name. She felt she was ready for a new one. The name Lightning, given by the old woman who'd originally adopted her, who'd rescued her from the cage at the cat prison, brought her to this house, and tenderly cared for her still healing wounds, was based, she knew, on the appearance of some marking on her face. (The old woman would stroke the mark and say her name.) But a physical characteristic was not a suitable basis for one's own name for oneself.

She sat on the upstairs landing, groomed her shoulder for a bit, then, when she had recovered her composure, she trotted into the back bedroom where the old lady who'd died had used to sleep. There she found an unusual scene.

Four cats—three females and one male—were all clumped together at the foot of the bed. Instead of dozing, they looked alert but unafraid. They were supposed to be there.

The young woman from the driveway appeared to be asleep on the bed, on her side, her knees pulled up, her skirt covering her feet. And in the rocking chair next to the bed sat the other ghost— the little hunched old woman Melancholy had recently seen hanging around the black dog's house.

As Melancholy entered the room, the old woman held a finger to her lips. "Shush," she said. "Mary Anne's asleep."

The cat padded over to the old woman and sat, looking up at her. The woman reached over and petted her. Or tried to. All the cat felt was a light cool breeze pulling at the tips of her hairs. She shuddered. "Sorry," the woman said. Then she looked at the bed.

"It was so sad," she mused, "that she died so long ago. And I had to live so long." She addressed Melancholy directly. "We were best friends." Melancholy thought of Lovey. "She lived here. I lived next door. She called me Winny, though my name is Winnifred. We used to run back and forth between our two houses. Until my baby brother's —" She stopped. "His accident changed everything. People were embarrassed when they saw me. Grownups, anyway. Children were just cruel. I dropped him, you see, out of an upstairs window. I was just showing him," she said sadly, "the sun and the lake. The *trees. And he turned in my hands and slipped away. My parents were kind people but they never got over it." She turned to look at Mary Anne. "At first Mary Anne and I tried to play the way we always had, but it wasn't any good. Eventually, we stopped visiting each other. She had her brothers. I had no one. And I stopped going out. It was too hard seeing people whisper and stare."*

Mary Anne muttered something and turned on the bed. The cats by her feet began to relax. Winnifred looked down at Mary Anne tenderly. "And so we grew up, separately. She helped her father in the store. Well, she was the eldest—four years older than John, six older than Alfred and seven older than Matthew—and her mother was busy with the boys. Even when they were little you could tell Alfred was Mary Anne's favourite. Her mother had Matthew almost right away after Alfred so Mary Anne kind of adopted him."

Winnifred laughed. "What a rapscallion he was! Always getting into places where he ought not to have been, making messes. But she loved him. They all did. He was the favourite. And then he went to war." Melancholy lay down near the ghost's feet, if a ghost could be said to have feet. She put her paws straight in front of her and purred quietly.

"By that time Mary Anne and I were both young ladies. We must have been—oh, about twenty or twenty-one when the war started, and were no longer speaking. Well, I hardly spoke to anyone anyway.

"I sometimes think my father let the thicket grow up between the two houses on purpose because he knew I liked to creep out there at night and listen to the Coneybear children playing and calling to each other in the garden.

"I remember there was a fever going around that spring. How cruel to die in spring after living through the long winter. Mary Anne caught the fever, we heard, and one night, the same night the telegram arrived telling them Alfred was missing in action—and everybody knew what that meant—she died."

Winnifred paused and stared into space. All the cats listened to her voice as if in a trance, their eyes every now and then slowly blinking, one ear or another giving the occasional twitch. "Where was I? Oh, yes. She died before she knew Alfred had been killed. And there was no body. The family didn't even have a funeral for him. Mary Anne's was bad enough, I heard. My parents went. Her father never got over losing two of his children on the same day. He went into a decline and died a few years later." She sank into a reverie again.

She looked down at Melancholy. "So she's stuck, you see? I can't reach her. Not yet. I've tried. But she's been waiting for him for so long, she can't stop. Will you help me?" She stretched out a wispy hand and again tried to stroke the cat's head.

Melancholy sat up and, looking directly into what might once have been the old woman's eyes, blinked once slowly, then again.

The woman sighed, then dissolved into nothing. For a few moments longer the rocking chair quivered.

21

*All is a clutter of narrow, crooked, dark, and dirty
lanes. (1792)*

Later, when Gerry looked back on that awful first week, driving
the boys back to Lovering to Mary's house once James was in
his cast, then rushing back to be by Doug's bedside as they waited
to see if he'd survive his injury and the surgery, it had been as if
she was weighted down. Her body, all five feet nothing of it, had
literally felt heavy. Her legs didn't want to lift her feet. Raising a cup
of coffee to her lips in the hospital canteen took a conscious effort.
Walking the halls of the hospital she felt as if she couldn't really
see, everything was so closed in. And focussing on what various
doctors said about Doug's condition was hard. She sometimes
had to ask them to repeat themselves, not because she didn't
understand what they were saying, but because she felt far away
from the sound of their voices, underwater, paddling mightily,
never quite surfacing.

After the first night and day, she got a hotel room and blessed
Prudence who'd advised her to pack some clothes and toiletries,
and who had thrust a travel mug full of the tea they'd not had a
chance to drink together into her trembling hand. Prudence had
held the fort cat-wise, biking to Gerry's twice a day to feed the
creatures and cleaning the house on Monday and Thursday just as
if everything was normal.

When, on the Friday after the accident, Doug opened his eyes briefly and seemed to recognize her, and Gerry had burst into tears, it was Prudence she phoned first, then Doug's sons. That Saturday the boys drove up with Mary in her car to visit Doug. Geoff drove and later David confided in Gerry that he'd gone ten kilometres below the speed limit, white-knuckling it the whole way, while his grandmother carped about his driving.

The second week had been less intense. Once Doug began talking and walking, the doctors lost interest, but in a good way, and by the end of the second Friday, and by dint of much pressuring of the staff on Gerry's part, she'd been able to get them to discharge him. She drove him to his own home where she delivered him to his sons. Friday night she returned home, cleaned the litter boxes and passed out under a pile of cats.

Now it was Monday morning; the third week of June was beginning. Glorious June. And Prudence was coming to clean.

Gerry stretched in bed and felt some of her tension release. She'd spent the weekend alternating sleeping with drawing. Four *Mug the Bug* comic strips were the result. And she'd sketched what she thought might be her next painting, a wide view of the lake, seen not from her house but from the large bay along the river road that led to the next town. The bay, with reedy shallows and insignificant sands, was the perfect backdrop for the five herons she'd spaced out, each in a distinctive hunting pose. She'd even found time to scribble in the tints she hoped to colour it with: watercolours, blue grey for the placid lake, a brighter hue for the herons, dull pale green for the reeds, sand for the sand (of course!) and the sky a washed-out blue beginning to be yellow-tinged in the far east.

She took a deep breath and stared out the window. The maples after which her house had been named were in full green leaf, and shaded her room from morning's light. She heard the birds, and a few cars driving by on Main Road. She heard the gentle rhythmic creak of a bicycle passing. The cats on her bed jumped off and ran to investigate.

That's Prudence arriving, Gerry sleepily thought, rolled over and went back to sleep. Prudence would feed the cats. Prudence would take care of everything.

She woke to the sound of the vacuum cleaner's relentless approach. It switched off and Prudence's head appeared in the doorway. "Are you ever going to wake up?"

"Don't say that!" Gerry said sharply, then, in a softer tone, "I'm sorry. It's just—I thought Doug wasn't going to." She smiled. "How are you?"

"*I'm* fine," Prudence huffed. "I just thought you might be getting hungry. There are blueberry pancakes in the oven keeping warm." She withdrew and restarted the vacuum.

Gerry rolled over. Eleven o'clock! And what a mess her room was in: dirty clothes everywhere. She certainly had spent a lazy weekend—housework-wise. Which apparently was over. She got out of bed, stepped past Prudence in the hallway and went for a shower. Prudence had vacuumed Gerry's room in the meantime, piling the clothes on her freshly made bed. Gerry dressed, bunged her laundry into the machine, then went to get her breakfast.

Upon entering the kitchen, she did a double take. There, on the counter, instead of the horrible old square black purse with the large brass snap fastener and short strap, was a soft woven shoulder bag in various shades of brown, cream and rust. Prudence had bought a new purse!

Prudence could be heard bringing the vacuum cleaner downstairs. She started in the bamboo room at the end of the house farthest from where Gerry sat at the living room table. When the brass mantelpiece clock (which had belonged to Gerry's mother) quietly ticked its way to twelve, the vacuum shut off and Gerry knew it was Prudence's lunchtime.

She, meanwhile, had been sorting two weeks' worth of bills and flyers, including Terry and Lucie's final bill. "So," she asked as Prudence sat down with her sandwich and bag of chips, "What's been going on?"

"The irises are out," her friend said.

"And?"

"And the poppies and some of the roses. And the gooseberries need to be picked. You could do that today." Prudence gave Gerry an assessing look. "If you're up to it."

"I'm up to it! I'm up to it! Your pancakes have given me the strength of ten women! What gives them that little crunch, by the way?"

Prudence looked smug. "I substitute one half cup of corn meal for one half cup of the flour."

"And they have oats in them too?"

Prudence nodded.

Gerry continued, "Yet they're light and fluffy. Nothing worse than a flat pancake, I always say."

"Because that would be a crêpe?" replied Prudence. "*You're* returning to normal."

Gerry exhaled a big sigh. "It's so good to be home. And to know Doug's safe at his home. I'm going to go over there later, but for now, besides the interesting doings in the garden—and yes, I will try to fit picking gooseberries into my busy afternoon—what's really been going on?"

"Well, in the neighbourhood, you mean?"

"With you and Bertie!" Gerry almost shouted. "Sorry. I see you bought a new purse. Very nice." Prudence said nothing, just smiled down at her lunch. Gerry sighed. "Okay, you win. Tell me about what the neighbours are doing. I know Blaise is back from his cruise. I saw his cats in my backyard, though when they saw Bob, Grey and Ariel beat a swift retreat back to Blaise's property. And Andrew and Markie are at Andrew's. I met Andrew at the hospital a couple of times. What about at Edwina's? Have you been over there?"

Prudence nodded. "The usual. The last two Fridays. Bless you people with pets, else I'd have much less work. She keeps a rag at the back door for Shadow's paws but she can't be remembering to use it all the time. The state of her floors!"

Gerry looked blank. "I'm not really interested in Edwina's *floors*, Prudence. You know. Any developments? Roald's murder? Anything?"

Prudence frowned. "She and I don't chat the way you and I do. I ask her how she is and how her writing is going, and if there are any special jobs she wants doing. Like that. Oh. One thing."

Gerry perked up. "Yes?"

"She hired a professional gardening company. In two days they trimmed shrubs, made garden beds and planted them with perennials and loads of annuals, and cordoned off parts of the yard so Shadow won't trample the grass seed."

"Wow! Not what I was expecting, but interesting. Why the rush?"

"She said she wants to have an open house at the end of June. She's joined the Lovering Garden Club so wants the outside of the house to look good, I guess."

"So you *do* talk," Gerry said accusingly.

"A bit. And I notice things. Her membership card for the garden club was on the counter. And I could hardly not comment when a team of ten gardeners descended on the place."

Gerry looked at her friend. She knew Prudence was squeamish about getting mixed up in murder. "Prudence, I'll ask you one more time. Any thoughts regarding Roald's murder? Any police sniffing around Edwina?"

"Not that I've seen," Prudence said, getting up. "She's more interested in her writing than anything. It's as if the books, at least while she's writing them, are where she really lives.

Everything else, like the dog, the house, the garden, is done grudgingly."

"That's a bit sad, don't you think?" queried Gerry.

"I really think it's just the way she is. And you know how distracted you get when you're drawing."

"You're right. I do. But I'm always glad to resurface back into my real life."

"Gerry," Prudence said softly. "That's because you have one."

And Gerry sat at the table looking out at the sunny day, counting her blessings.

"Ouch!" she said for the hundredth time. The gooseberry shrub was defending its fruit. "Nobody told me about the thorns!" she grumbled, stripping the red-tinged green berries that hung from drooping prickly branches. "And you can stop looking so smug!" she told Bob, who was innocently supervising from a nearby patch of soil.

He rolled on his back, having a dirt bath, and daring her to rub his tummy. Of course she did.

Prudence had advised her to wear long sleeves and pants, but Gerry, hungry for the sun after the last two weeks spent either in the hospital or her car, had chosen a tank top and short shorts. "Next time I'll listen," she muttered. "She always knows best."

A bird called nearby and Bob jerked to a half sitting position then took off into the underbrush. "Fine," Gerry called. "I'll finish the rest myself."

But the sun did feel good on her arms and legs and she soon filled the big plastic bowl Prudence had given her. She straightened her back and looked around the garden.

Designed in a series of rectangular beds with narrow paths between, it was looking spectacular. The petals of poppies, in various shades of pink, salmon, orange and tomato, fluttered softly in the breeze. Irises, the poppies' stiff companions, projected green spears topped with blue flowers, purple flowers, yellow and white flowers, and a curious colour which could, if one were being kind, be described as mahogany, or unkind, mud. And the roses!

The roses were opening, some boldly—big, bright colours—and some shyly—little buds becoming small palest pink or ivory blooms.

Gerry took a look at her vegetable garden and then looked again. Beans! She had bean plants! Six inches high already. Likewise the edible podded peas and the scarlet runner beans, though some of the latter, around their teepee of poles, had been nibbled, probably by rabbits. Brave rabbits, considering the number of cats patrolling the property daily. And there were two rows of tiny carrot greens an inch high. Gerry sighed with satisfaction. Things beginning. Spring. The hospital was already receding from her memory. She took her gooseberries into the house.

22

With the red mantle of their cluttered blood. (1577)

While the rhubarb and gooseberry chutney (which also contained onions and apples, raisins, dark brown sugar and vinegar, and an array of strong spices) was bubbling on the stove, Gerry returned to the table to finish sorting her mail. An envelope from the Canadian government made her pause. "I did my taxes," she protested. Something small, flat and hard was in the envelope. She ripped it open and peered in, then shook a small red disc into her hand. "Oh," she breathed out softly, and read the accompanying letter.

From the Commonwealth War Graves Commission, it informed her that as she was a Coneybear and resided at the same address of one Alfred Coneybear, deceased, it had been decided that she was the appropriate next of kin to be notified that his tags had been found with those of two other Canadian soldiers who were part of Canadian forces defending the Ypres Salient in the spring of 1915. They regretted they could not provide any information about the exact day of death but that the remains had been interred in a cemetery in France—the Loos British Cemetery—and that the name of Alfred Coneybear, as she might or might not know, was already inscribed on the Menin Gate Memorial in West Flanders along with the names of the other fallen.

Gerry put down the letter and held the little tag, feeling a lump come into her throat. Then she put it and the letter on the mantel and went to check the chutney.

Its vinegar steam seemed to be making her eyes water and she was blowing her nose when Prudence entered the kitchen. "Allergies?"

"No," said Gerry, feeling for some reason that she wanted to keep the letter about Alfred private, just for a little while. "The vinegar and mustard seed, I guess. Shall I prepare the jars?"

Prudence gave her a keen look, then nodded. "Yes. It looks almost ready."

They decanted the chutney into hot clean jars and Gerry screwed on the lids. Then they sat down to tea. Prudence had brought rhubarb streusel muffins from her house.

"Don't tell me you also have a giant rhubarb plant in your backyard?" Gerry quizzed her.

"No. This is from your garden. Maggie used to let me have as much as I wanted so I took some while you were away. Is that all right?"

"Of course! Take some gooseberries while you're at it."

"Thank you. I will. And I'll bring you some of the jam I make from them. Scented with a bit of orange peel and juice."

After tea, Prudence finished her day's work and pedalled home. Gerry washed and changed and drove over to see Doug.

His car had been destroyed, so she wasn't surprised to see a rental in the driveway. She knocked and was let in by David. They hugged. Doug was lying on one of the living room's two sofas, looking pale and tired. The hair on one side of his head was gone. He sat up and smiled. "Hello, love. How nice to see you." They kissed and Gerry sat next to him. She could hear the sound of the television coming from the little room off the kitchen-dining-living room.

"Dad, you need anything?" David called from the kitchen where he was organizing cans of pop and a giant jar of dry roasted peanuts.

"No, son. You enjoy your time with your brothers." David tactfully closed the TV room door behind him. "The locusts are still feeding," Doug laughed.

Gerry gave Doug a real kiss, then sank back on the sofa. "Growing boys and all that. I got caught up with Mug, and Prudence showed me how to make chutney. I'm exhausted! The woman is relentless!"

Doug looked at her fondly. "She was probably trying to distract you."

"From what?"

He touched his bandaged head. "From this, I expect."

She touched it carefully. "How does it feel?"

"Fine. See? That's what Prudence saw. Your face scrunched up and you sounding worried. I'm getting better. And it's summer. Well, not officially, but close enough."

"Why don't we…" Gerry began slowly. "Why don't we go upstairs and see just how better you're feeling?"

He smiled and let her lead him.

23

They clutter and run and rise and escape from him. (1824)

As Gerry drove home late that night, a couple of things were bothering her, one of which was—who had killed Roald Henderson?

When she got out of her car she listened for frogs as she always did at night. What she heard were terrible feline growls coming from behind Blaise's house. She trotted across the lawn. "Bob! Bob!" she called urgently in a low voice. The growling stopped, then resumed in full force with some hissing added in.

"Is that you, Gerry?" came Blaise's quavery voice.

"Yes, Blaise. I'm just trying to catch my bad cat." She could just make out the two male cats, who'd always hated each other, vying for top cat position when Graymalkin (a.k.a. Stupid) had been one of Aunt Maggie's and then Gerry's cats. One grey, one black and white, both angry, they crouched, facing each other, ears flat and tails thrashing. Soon there would be tears.

"Hang on," Blaise responded, disappearing into his kitchen, then reappearing at the sliding glass doors. He snapped open a can of cat food and the growling ceased. Gerry saw Graymalkin's svelte form run towards Blaise and enter the house. Blaise slid the door almost closed and said, "That's done it. You're out late."

As she caught a now foolish-looking Bob, she said, "I was over at Doug's. He's much better. Did you know he'd had an accident?"

"Yes," her neighbour replied. "Cathy told me. I'm glad he's recovering."

"How was your cruise?"

"Lovely. I must have gained five pounds."

"Oh well, you're so skinny, you can afford to. I'll come visit soon and hear all about it, okay?"

"Okay. 'Night."

"'Night." She walked back to her house, cradling Bob and murmuring words of love into his ears. "Oh, Bob, were you defending our castle from the hideous monster Graymalkin? Who's a good cat?" Kiss, kiss, kiss.

Surprisingly, Bob did not retch from this sickening display, nor did he try to escape from her arms. Possibly he agreed with her. Or possibly, he was fixating on what was happening on the other side of their property. By the sound of crunching gravel, one could tell a car was slowly entering Edwina Murray's driveway. Gerry stopped rubbing her chin on Bob's head and looked where he was looking.

Even in the dark it was possible to tell the car was a bright yellow and low slung. It looked tough and expensive. The boy who quietly got out of it and carefully closed its door looked the same—jeans, white tee, leather jacket, black boots.

Gerry froze. Now what?

The boy went to Edwina's back door and quietly knocked. The door opened and he went in.

Gerry's mind was a blank. Who was he? Then something clicked and she remembered the yellow car she'd seen from the ferry almost a month earlier. Seen in almost the same spot in Edwina's driveway. Was this the man who had seemed to be having a disagreement with Andrea before driving away? "Huh," she said to Bob. "Huh. I have no idea what's going on, do I?" His quiet purr told her he didn't care if she did or didn't. They went in to bed.

How long she slept, she never knew, though it seemed but a moment, because the next thing she was aware of was waking to hear the sound of another car arriving at Edwina's. But this one's driver didn't bother to try to arrive discreetly. As its driver slammed on the brakes, the tires protested as they left a bit of themselves on the road. "What?" she said, sitting up. She imagined the spray of gravel when it stopped on the driveway. Her little crew of cats likewise all stirred. "I don't like it," she mumbled, slipping into her Winnie-the-Pooh robe and going downstairs.

She put on her rubber boots and grabbed a flashlight. After letting herself out, she paused for a moment near the shed. Andrea's gun was still in there, she thought doubtfully. If she needed it. She shook her head, decided to leave the gun where it was, and slowly walked through the thicket to Edwina's back garden. She was vaguely aware of Bob, Jay, Lightning and Seymour following her.

The professional gardeners had certainly done their jobs. The new flower beds were a riot of colours—even at night—plants tightly placed side by side. It was not to Gerry's taste but she supposed it was impressive.

She failed to notice a string stretched between two pegs low down and found herself face down inspecting the burgeoning new grass. "Rats," she whispered to Seymour who gently rubbed against her head, and scrambled to her feet, feeling foolish. The group of cats, now augmented by the addition of Mother, the boys and Ronald, all looked at her as if they couldn't believe the clumsiness of bipeds.

She managed to get herself near the closest car—a red convertible Mercedes, sleek and lovely. Andrea's. Gerry remembered her backing it into Edwina's fence and saw the damaged rear fender. Then she drew near the yellow car, chunky and powerful looking. A Mustang, she noted. Vintage, by the look of it.

From there, she carefully crunched over the gravel to the back wall of the house. Where before there had been simply weeds and garbage cans, there was now a raised planter with some stiff flowers in it in hard reds and pinks—zinnias?—and no sign of the cans. She moved along the edge of the planter to the door. The cats—all nine of them—similarly edged.

She heard a noise from inside the house and moved back, inadvertently stepping on one of Winston's paws. He yowled. "Shush!" she hissed. Inside the house, Shadow barked once but that was all. Gerry and the cats waited.

Then Bob streaked past the door and under the kitchen windows. Some of the cats followed him while some hung back with Gerry. Feeling ridiculous (accompanied by cats!—what good could they do?), yet also kind of enjoying herself (after all, she could always claim she was chasing cats!), Gerry crept near the windows. The kitchen was brightly lit.

Reasoning that when one was inside a lighted room it was difficult to see out into the dark, she carefully peeked into the room. It was empty. She swore. By now Bob was past the kitchen and approaching the window of Edwina's study, beneath which someone had planted a row of lupins—pink, blue, and yellow cones. Fine, thought Gerry, expeditionary forces led by Captain Bob with assorted cats next, then me.

Bob sat below the window looking up. Gerry was almost that far along the back of the house, crouching over, when Shadow started barking. She heard a door slam inside the house, then a yelp and silence. The yelp made her uneasy. She straightened, then looked carefully into Edwina's study.

Because she was only seeing one side of the room, the only person she could make out was Edwina, her back to the wall, sitting behind her desk. She looked pale but resolute. That she was listening to other people was evident from the faint murmur of voices that leaked through the closed window.

Edwina must have caught a glimpse of Gerry moving because she got up from her desk and opened the window a crack. "It's a bit hot in here," she said, briefly making eye contact with Gerry. Edwina didn't seem frightened so Gerry waited. A woman who must be Andrea was speaking to the mystery boy and she sounded on the verge of hysteria. Good thing her gun was safely in Gerry's shed, she thought. And who was he? Another one of her boyfriends?

"So what you're telling me, Johnny, is that it was an accident that you shot Roald? And that then you tried to frame his wife? Well? Talk to me, Johnny!"

Gerry tried to keep calm. At her feet, some of the cats, growing restless, moved away. Mother began to dig in a nearby flowerbed of pink daisies. Ronald began a game with Joseph. Bob, to Gerry's horror, jumped up onto the windowsill.

"What's that?" said a young male voice, presumably that of Johnny.

Edwina replied calmly. "My neighbour, believe it or not, has, er, about twenty cats. That's one of them." Bob sat down, looking at the garden, seemingly unconcerned with the activity within the house.

"Must be a nut," said the voice. Bob turned and looked a bit offended, and Gerry, despite what she was hearing, felt a wild desire to laugh.

"Johnny, I need to know what happened," Andrea repeated.

There was the scrape of chair legs on floor and Gerry guessed that someone had taken a seat. Andrea entered her frame of vision and sat on something under the window, the back of her head to Gerry. The boy began talking.

"You and Roald got back from that party that was here that Friday night. The one I wasn't invited to. You were both hammered.

Then you must have gone up to bed and taken one of your pills, or passed out, because Roald came into the living room alone. And we started drinking. Then I showed him my gun." A stifled exclamation came from Andrea but she said nothing. "Then he went out to his car and got his gun. He kept it there because *she* didn't like having it in the house." His voice became whiny. "I followed him outside and I was holding his gun and it just went off. The fool kept it loaded."

There was a silence as the two women, three, if you counted Gerry, digested this information. He's lying, thought Gerry. She no longer felt like laughing.

Edwina broke the silence. "He must have been afraid of the loan sharks."

Then Andrea spoke, sounding perplexed. "But I thought *I* had your dad's gun." Oh my God, thought Gerry, he's her son. "Which has disappeared," she added, with an uneasy look in Edwina's direction.

"You did." Now he sounded smug. "I bought my own. They're easy to find. I got it through one of Roald's friends. Funny, eh?"

He must have taken it out because Andrea hissed, "Put it away, Johnny!"

There was a silence, then Edwina said, "Not funny at all, you horrible boy. Horrifying. Why did you take Roald's body to the churchyard?"

"Going to put me in one of your mystery books?" he sneered.

"I might," Edwina replied serenely, "if you're interest-ing enough."

This seemed to make him think, for he paused. Then he said, sulkily, "I remembered sneaking a joint there after Dad's funeral, and it's near our house. I used Roald's own car to move him—well, he'd dropped right next to the open trunk. I'd have to have been an idiot not to use it. Then after I dumped the body, I drove the car back here."

"How did you get home?" Edwina's asked curiously. "It's quite a few miles and somebody might have seen you walking late at night."

"Took the tracks. Had a bit of a fright when I came upon the body. It had fallen all the way down the cliff."

Andrea lowered her head and disappeared from Gerry's sight. I bet she's holding it in her hands, Gerry thought. She must be reeling. Talk about chickens coming home to roost.

Edwina's cool tones cut through the tension in the room. "And what are you going to do now?"

He must have made a threatening move because Andrea stood up quickly. She moved away from the window, putting herself between Edwina and her son. "No, Johnny!"

"Why not, Mum? It's not as if you like her or anything. We could type a suicide note on that thing." He must mean Edwina's computer, Gerry thought. "And leave the gun with her fingerprints on it." He mimicked his mother's voice. "'She's in the way. Why won't she divorce him?' But she never would, would she? And he wouldn't leave her and all her money. Did he already have your replacement ready, Mum? Really, I did you a favour. Both of you."

"That's enough, John." Andrea took a step towards him. "You could plead it was an accident for Roald's death but not this. Give me the gun." Gerry's skin tightened on the back of her neck. Bob, much to her relief, jumped off the windowsill and busied himself under a nearby shrub.

But his sudden motion must have startled Johnny because he fired at the window then rushed over to it. Gerry sank to the ground amidst broken glass. Lupins snapped. The cats had scattered. So much for my troops, she thought. Her ears rang from the shot.

"What?" roared Edwina. "Another window? You've got to be kidding me. Get out! Get out!"

The next thing Gerry knew, Johnny and Andrea were exiting Edwina's house. She sprinted around to the far side of it and waited until she heard both their engines start and then leave the property. She looked toward the road. Both vehicles, the red following the yellow, drove towards central Lovering. She peeked around the corner of the house.

"Hadn't you better come in?" Edwina's voice called wearily from the space where the window's glass had been.

24

A solitary Privacy far from the rustling clutterments
of the tumultuous and confused World. (1693)

"Really, he *did* do me a favour," Edwina said quietly. Not wanting to attract mosquitoes in through the shattered window space, she'd closed the door to her study, released Shadow from imprisonment in Roald's den, where, she explained, Johnny had put him when he'd arrived, and met Gerry at the back door.

Silently, Gerry handed Edwina a snapped-off lupin. It was yellow. Edwina dropped it into a glass of water.

They sat in the kitchen sipping tea.

"My cats may jump in your broken window," Gerry said. "Especially Bob. He's been in here before, last winter, mostly with me, I expect."

"As long as he or they go out again. I forget—what were you doing in the house?"

"I think I told you. Looking for one of Blaise Parminter's cats."

"Oh. Yes. Well, what a strange series of events. Let me see if I understand it." Edwina ticked points off on her fingers.

"One. Johnny is Andrea's son by her first husband. He doesn't care for husband number two, who she divorces anyway, and only slightly tolerates her subsequent lover—Roald.

"Two. He realizes his mother wishes to marry Roald. For some reason. Do you think it was for the money he'd have gotten from divorcing me?"

Gerry spoke slowly. "That depends, Edwina. How much are you worth? If you don't mind my asking."

"For a long time, not much," Edwina said grimly. "Then the last two books took off. They got international distribution. I guess that increased revenue made Roald even less inclined to leave me. He'd have waited as long as he could, to get his half." She added under her breath, "Waited too long, it seems. How many numbers was I up to?"

"Three is next," Gerry said drily.

"But I haven't finished two. Andrea seems to have money. Look at the cars they drive."

"Rich people can never have too much money," Gerry said, thinking, I sound positively wise.

"Mmm. So. Three. Either deliberately or by accident, Johnny shoots Roald, disposes of his body and makes it safely back to his house.

"Four. Uh, he gets afraid when the police don't arrest me and leaves the gun under the car in my driveway, where it's found." Gerry cleared her throat. "Yes?" Edwina asked.

"Who found the gun?"

"I did. I handed it over to the police when they came the first time."

Gerry looked disbelievingly at Edwina. She'd handed the police the murder weapon, probably with her fingerprints on it. Edwina didn't seem to notice Gerry's incredulity and continued.

"Five. Johnny backs off when he hears I'm detained at the police station, but his mother, after shooting out one of my windows, is convinced of my innocence and begins to look more closely at her son. Maybe, she thinks, he used his father's gun, which she thought she'd safely hidden, probably in her room.

She, too, at least for a while, probably thinks of framing me, if she suspects her only child of the murder. No? Boy, number five is sure getting long."

"I don't think what's been happening between Andrea and her son is going to be clear to anyone but them," offered Gerry. "And is probably still happening right now at their house. Maybe it'll all be obvious in the morning. Is it still Monday?"

Edwina looked at the clock over Gerry's head. "I'm afraid not. But I'm not tired. I've got to get some of this down on paper or else I won't be able to sleep."

And there Gerry left her, still counting on her fingers the points to be listed.

Gerry wanted to sleep in but got no support for this idea from the cats who woke her promptly at eight. She grumblingly fed them, did the litter boxes, then went back to bed. She didn't get up until noon, then spent the afternoon working on her painting of the five herons. That's what I'll call it, she thought—*Fishing*.

She took her mid-afternoon coffee out on to the back porch with the fifth Swallows and Amazons book—*Coot Club*. She told herself, just one more chapter, before I go work on *Mug*, and fell asleep.

She was aboard the *Teasel* with Dick and Dot and old Mrs. Barrable and William the pug, and they were adrift. The small sailing vessel went slowly down one of the Norfolk Broads. Slowly, at first, then faster and faster, until the *Teasel* began to turn. Soon she was spinning wildly, the pug was barking and Mrs. Barrable was saying, "We really shouldn't be here," when Gerry awoke.

She felt dizzy. Andrew and Markie were walking away across the lawn. "Wait! I'm awake! Wait!" They turned, she beckoned and they began walking back. "Oh!" she said, when they were near, "I don't know what's wrong with me. I'm so sleepy. Hello."

"Hello!" Andrew said. "We won't stay. We just wanted to thank you for stepping up when Doug and the boys needed you. I couldn't leave Arizona; we were so close to finishing packing Markie's stuff."

Gerry blinked at the couple standing on the lawn. "So you're here for good now, Markie?"

Markie smiled. "Yup. My movers won't arrive for another week but I'm here." She nudged Andrew. "Go on."

Andrew cleared his throat nervously. "Ah, Gerry. We were wondering if we could, if you would allow us—"

"What Andy's trying to say is, can we get married here, on your back lawn?" Markie gestured around her. "It's the combination of the lake and the garden. It's just lovely."

"We'd arrange for and pay for everything," Andrew said anxiously. "Especially if something was damaged."

Markie continued, "All you have to do is show up. And maybe be the maid of honour."

"I would love to be your maid of honour," Gerry said slowly, "and you can have the garden. Of course you can. We're family. Er, when were you thinking?"

"Early August?" Andrew said.

Gerry nodded. "Yes. Why not? Are you sure you won't come in?"

"Not tonight," Markie replied. "We're going over to Cathy's to discuss the menu. She'll cater the wedding, of course."

"Of course," Gerry echoed. "Well, you've certainly given me lots to think about. And congratulations!"

"Thank you," they chorused. Markie added, "I'll be in touch about your dress." The two walked away hand in hand.

"Dress? Oh, yeah, a dress." Gerry sat looking at the garden, trying to envisage where a large tent might go, where they would serve the food and drink, how to set up lights if the party were to continue on into the evening, and what to do about the hordes of mosquitoes that were sure to descend at dusk.

And the cats. What about the cats? She pictured Ronald or possibly Jay running up Markie's wedding gown, getting claws caught in her veil. Her mind digressed. I wonder if she will wear a classic dress and veil. Well, the shy cats will hide and the curious ones will mingle and no doubt there will be some unfortunate incidents, but nothing we won't be able to handle. An angry yowl from outside the porch reminded her it was cat suppertime.

She wasn't hungry herself, so wandered through the house, stopping in the dining room in front of the store. Time to turn this into a proper nook, she thought.

She dragged all the wooden casks and boxes out of the little room and surveyed the limited space. The desk at the far end would stay, of course, and its chair. Next she went into the bamboo room and looked at an old green brocade chaise longue with a carved wooden armrest that curved up and around the top of the back of the chaise. She encouraged herself: I can move this, and bit by bit dragged it through the hallway and dining room to position it along the right-hand wall of the nook, facing the desk.

"Whew, that was hard work," she told Seymour and Lightning, who had joined her and were also surveying the room. "Now for the smaller stuff."

She brought three casks back in and set them up on their ends a few feet apart along the window wall. Then she went out to the shed and rummaged around in her limited collection of leftover timber. "Aha!" She dragged the piece of plywood into the house and laid it atop the casks. "I can paint this and, or, cover it in cloth. And one of these—" She fetched one of the old crates and set it next to the chaise longue. "Voila! My side table."

She sat on the chaise and mimed taking a drink off the crate. Seymour jumped up onto her lap. Lightning paced around the room, then settled on the new "table" under the window.

Gerry let her head fall back and looked out the window. High up, it offered only a view of trees, a bit of evening sky. Perfect, she thought. No lake, nothing really distracting, just a little nook where I can come when I want to read or think. Or dream, a little voice added.

She roused herself and reluctantly left the nook, made a few trips taking the leftover casks and crates out to the garage. She walked through the length of the garage into the little potting shed that was tacked onto the street side of the building.

The two remaining catnip plants flourished in their west-facing window. She stroked the soft leaves and smelled their slightly minty odour. They'd have to stay inside in safety all summer. Then, the plan was to dry the catnip and dole it out to the cats indoors over the winter. Maybe she'd make her own catnip mice.

She went back inside, pausing by the open fireplace in the living room. Did she really want to close it off, replace it with a wood stove? She remembered the cozy warmth radiating from her friend Jean-Louis's stove this past winter. But surely, now the house was well insulated, she could keep her lovely large brick fireplace?

Wait. She walked into the dining room and peered at its smaller black wrought iron hearth. Does this still work? No one's said it does or doesn't. What if I put a wood stove in here? She grew excited. It's in the centre of the house, under the bedrooms, next to the nook. A perfect position to radiate warmth. I'll ask Prudence. I'll ask Doug. I bet I'd save money on oil by burning wood instead. And be more ecological. It's a thought.

She re-entered the nook and turned on the desk lamp. Already the little space was looking less like a store. She felt a pang of loss. Then she walked around the house gathering a few things she thought belonged in the nook. She arranged them, some in the post office pigeonholes on the wall next to the chaise longue, some on the desk, and some, just for now, until she could get a few frames, tacked to the wall above the desk. There, she thought, that's better.

25

I've seed strange things in my time, but this clutters me! (1888)

Gerry pulled on the bug hat, lowered its net and squirted it and herself liberally with citronella insect repellent. It smelled nice, kind of. Adding an old pair of running shoes to her ensemble of baggy pants tucked into socks, and a long-sleeved flannel shirt, she felt she was ready for a walk in the woods. She hadn't been in ages.

She passed in front of Andrew's (and now Markie's) house. Markie was shaking out a doormat. The hand that held a stiff brush paused as she spied Gerry in her mosquito and tick-proof gear.

Gerry waved and kept going. She passed the Coneybear family crypt and turned up the long dirt road that led past Cathy's B&B.

Cathy was out with Prince Charles on his leash. The basset-beagle cross, catching sight of the weird apparition that was Gerry, let out a series of the odd braying noises that passed for his barks.

Gerry likewise saluted Cathy, shouting a brief hello, and then entered the shady portion of the lane, at the end of which was a farmhouse, usually empty, but now, with two cars parked at the side, obviously inhabited.

Gerry dithered. In winter and fall, she just tromped across the house's lawn. She paused next to a barbed wire fence, then, being too short to simply swing a leg over it, she lifted the top wire and pushed down on the middle wire, trying to insert herself through the space in between.

This strategy, which had worked in other seasons and elsewhere, failed her today. The bug hat caught on the upper wire and the lower wire snagged her pants. Imagining the inhabitants of the farmhouse, whom she did not know, watching this performance from behind curtains, it was a hot and embarrassed Gerry who extricated herself a few minutes later. She hoped this walk would be worth it. She needed to think.

She skirted the edge of the field until she was past the house and at the point where the path trailed away into the woods. She wondered if she should list points on her fingers as Edwina had. But Gerry's was a free-ranging mind, so she just let things come into and out of her head as they appeared.

First, she supposed she should examine her feelings on receiving a call from Dr. Barron that morning. She'd been planning a happy day of drawing and gardening when the phone had rung. What Dr. Barron, who'd first apologized for the delay, and who was just getting back to her practice, had told her, was going to change her life. It certainly explained her tiredness, dizziness, even her allergies, which the doctor had suggested might be temporary. And the fact that wine didn't taste good to her anymore.

She got to the tracks and, as always, paused. To the left, an hour away by train, was Montreal. To the right, a short walk away, was Lovering's tiny business district. She thought of Johnny, having killed a man, walking the tracks in the middle of the night. Despite his recent bluster in front of his mother and Edwina, he was still a boy. How terrified he must have been. He was Andrea's son. How could he have gone so wrong? She wondered where he was now.

She crossed the tracks and immediately felt calmer. The woods were cooled and darkened by the immense maples that covered the side of the hill. There was the family's sugar shack. She supposed that Andrew or Mary must own it now. She wondered if they would someday repair it, replace the rusting maple-sugar-making equipment inside, run lines from trees to shack, make maple syrup again.

She climbed the hill. The rutted path, stones and gravel exposed in places by rain and the spring run-off of melting snow, was rough or mucky, depending. She made it up the slope and paused again to listen.

Birds fluttered and called, insects hummed, and a little in the distance she heard the voices of golfers on the nearby course.

The woods darkened even more as she entered the pine plantation, planted by Uncle Geoff years and years ago. She sat on a fallen limb and thought of Doug.

What would *he* say? He who'd just had a brush with death; whose three sons teetered on the brink of adulthood. Would he be upset? Angry, even?

She sighed. She would have to tell him soon. Him. And Prudence.

But what do *you* feel, Gerry? she asked herself. She smiled slowly. Happy, she thought. I feel happy.

After a leisurely walk home and an equally leisurely lunch on the back porch, she decided to go shopping.

In Lovering's grocery store she wandered slowly up and down the aisles, taking things off the shelves, reading labels, putting them back or keeping them—a new type of tea, a carton of squash soup, an ash-covered cheese—all the while, in another part of her brain, daydreaming.

When she got to the fruit and vegetable department, she lingered by the tomatoes, then finally picked one up, saying softly, "How about you? Would you like to come home with me?"

An elderly woman, also looking at tomatoes, didn't miss a beat, just said, "You have to talk to them, don't you?"

Gerry laughed. "Well, yes." She paused. The woman had a nice face. "I'm Gerry."

"Beulah," said the woman. "Beulah—"

"Postlethwaite!" said a surprised Gerry.

The woman looked surprised. "How do you know my name?"

After Gerry explained, flushing at her presumption, that her aunt, when a little girl in the 1950s, had written a story in which a Beulah Postlethwaite, one of the minister's daughters, appeared, and Gerry had assumed that such an unusual name wouldn't be that common, er, um—Beulah rescued her from her confusion. "Yes, it is unusual, isn't it? My father named me. It means 'promised land.' What's the story about?"

"It's about him, actually. Would you like to read it?" They exchanged phone numbers and promised to meet.

At home Gerry unpacked her purchases and tried the new tea—vanilla. Not bad, she thought. Makes a change from Earl Grey.

She sat on the steps outside the side porch, basking in the late afternoon sun and idly watching Seymour and Lightning at their post by the potting shed door.

"Gerry?"

She looked up and held her hand to shield her eyes from the sun. Edwina was standing in the driveway, her cheeks tear-stained.

"I don't want to bother you again, but I thought you should know, Andrea just phoned me to say Johnny had turned himself in."

Gerry patted the step next to her. Edwina sat. "Why were you crying?" she asked quietly.

"The relief. I know I seem detached, but that's just my coping mechanism. I knew the evidence against me was pretty bad. I mean good. Good for the police. Bad for me." She sighed. "I wish I could mourn Roald more. But I can't."

After a moment Gerry changed the subject. "How's Norman doing? Is he or the case against him still crumbling?"

"He's dead," Edwina replied flatly. "But I changed it again. His wife didn't kill him. It was his best friend."

Gerry nodded. "I never thought she did."

Edwina stood up. "All right then. Did Prudence tell you I'm having a garden party soon?"

"She did."

"You're both invited. Well, the next book won't write itself. I'm calling it *Wild Blood*. See you."

"See you." Gerry wondered what on earth—oh, of course—Edwina's next book would probably feature a young man going wrong. Wild blood. She finished her tea and walked out onto the lawn. At its edges, patches of blue forget-me-nots and white lilies of the valley competed for space. There was a hot mauve geranium that must have escaped from the perennial garden, and two types of Solomon's seal that dripped either with flowers of creamy foam or dangling bells. In a sunny patch, orange paintbrushes were starting to show.

In the thicket between The Maples and Edwina's house, wild roses and raspberries bloomed. The violets under them had long faded, but she could still see a few hellebore flowers flaunting their strong dusky pink.

And down by the water wild daisies and clover, buttercups and fleabane competed with tall grasses.

She looked toward the perennial garden to her right, where a few stalks of yellow loosestrife pricked the eye. As did a mostly purple vista with lilac-coloured low-growing phlox, and the globes of alliums, flowering onions, nestled to one side of a bed of iris.

It would all look so different by early August, by the time of Markie and Andrew's wedding. All these colours today would have faded. But others would have sprung up to take their places.

Gerry wasn't an experienced enough gardener to know what those plants and colours might be, but she knew some at least of the old roses would still be blooming, roses, many of them, planted by her ancestors.

She walked a little further down the lawn toward the lake. The soaring maples and, behind them, the golden willow that hung over the pool, cast a deep shade. Beneath the trees, wood anemone sported its white stars.

She thought of all the paintings she would make. Fireflies in the trees and over the lawn at night. Her cats, dotted about the landscape. The wild geese and ducks, gathering in great squadrons in the fall. A blue jay on her windowsill on a bright winter day, cocking its head curiously.

She thought of all the good things she and Prudence would make together using the fruits of her garden: the strawberry, raspberry, blueberry jams; the pies; the black currant and crab apple jellies. She thought of the herbs she would dry for winter's soups and stews, then paused her itinerary and grinned. That was, if she ever had the time or inclination to make any soups and stews instead of eternally heating up frozen or canned food!

She walked out onto the little promontory, twenty feet of rocks tossed to make a rough pier, and sat. All around her, playing, rising and falling in the last sliver of the setting sun's light that streamed through the space between her house and shed, were hundreds of orange butterflies the size of her thumbnail.

She spread her arms toward the lake. The butterflies danced. And she laughed with joy.

ovey followed Melancholy to the shed by the road. She was changing. He could tell she was getting stronger by the quality of her purr, which he heard and felt when they slept close together. It was steadier. It was good.

They passed the girl who fed them, sitting on the steps at the side of the house, and approached the young woman in the mauve dress.

The other woman, old and hunched over, wafted over the shed roof, coming from the house where the black dog lived. She alighted on the pavement of the parking pad and gestured with her hand at the two cats.

Melancholy sat close to Mary Anne and began rubbing against her ankles. Lovey did the same on the other side. Both cats were startled when the woman who lived with the black dog came around the corner of the shed and almost stepped on them.

She had a brief conversation with their girl, then left. The girl disappeared behind the house. The cats tried again to get Mary Anne's attention.

Both of them reared up, batting at her flowing skirts. They were baffled when their claws snagged only on air.

Melancholy sat down. This wasn't going to work. She looked at Winnifred, who was circling her friend, likewise trying to get through to her. But to no avail.

Winnifred looked imploringly at the cats. Melancholy heard her words inside her own head. Please try again, Winnifred pleaded. We can't leave her here forever. Soon she'll just blow away.

It was true. They could see Mary Anne's smoky essence was thinning and dissipating. Melancholy didn't know what would happen to the ghost if she blew away, but she knew it wouldn't be good.

Lovey, disturbed by the distress of Winnifred and inattentiveness of Mary Anne, crouched, crossed his paws, and tucked them away under his chest. He dozed. It was up to Melancholy.

She walked over to where he sat and arranged herself in a similar posture. She closed her eyes and began concentrating, directing all her energy into two words—Mary Anne.

She felt the flames licking at her hind legs, burning off her tail. She ignored them. She ignored the pain and the sound of the jeering drunken men who'd tried to kill her. Their voices grew faint. She heard Lovey's purr next to her and added her own.

All the while, Winnifred also was calling, "Mary Anne, Mary Anne." She floated in front of her friend's face, catching at her hands.

And then the cats and Winnifred knew their work had been enough. All three stopped their cries and thoughts and let go of their combined energies. The cats opened their eyes. Butterflies fluttered around the two ghosts.

Slowly Mary Anne looked at her friend from long ago. "Winny? Winny. How did you get so old?" Then she looked around her and said, "I'm waiting for Alfred. He's gone to war. I haven't had a letter from him for weeks."

"Oh, my dear," Winnifred said, with sorrowful pity in her voice. "He's not coming home. I'm so sorry. Here, let me show you." Gently, she led Mary Anne around to the back of the house, where the outline of the blocked-up door to the post office and store was still visible.

The cats followed the women, watched them pass through the door, then themselves darted through the cat flap and into the dining room. They sat at the opening to the store.

Winnifred led Mary Anne over to the old desk. Both the ghosts sighed as they looked at the little red tag on the desk, the photograph of a young man, and a letter and newspaper cutting, both framed, hanging above the desk.

Then Mary Anne, catching sight of a little box containing two figures—the man dressed all in beige, the woman in a long mauve dress—and two cats—one a tailless tortoiseshell, the other one-eyed with short black fur—gave a little cry and was embraced by Winnifred.

Lovey followed Melancholy back outside. It was still light out. Butterflies surrounded the girl down by the water. The two cats settled underneath the plant with enormous leaves and listened to evening fall. Each groomed the other's face. Then Melancholy told Lovey her new name.

ACKNOWLEDGEMENTS

For the history of a certain town that resembles Lovering quite a lot, I visited the online site of the Hudson Historical Society. Of particular value was the timeline compiled and written by Maben Poirier.

The letter written by Alfred Coneybear was based on a real letter written by Percy Leland Kingsley, born 1886, who survived Ypres and lived a long, and one hopes, happy life, dying at the age of ninety-six in 1982. I found it at greatwaralbum.ca. I hope he wouldn't mind my paraphrasing it in this book.

As always, a shout-out to The Greenwood Centre for Living History in Hudson, Quebec, known locally as Greenwood House (a.k.a. The Maples), for being the place I chose to settle Gerry.

A WORD ABOUT SANDY

And now it's time to mention Sandy, to whom this book is dedicated.

About a year before I began writing this book, my daughter heard about a stray cat who had been found in January's biting cold and was being kept in a garage. She went to look at it and fell in love. At the vets' we were told the cat had frostbite on his back legs. So we treated those. But someone slipped up, and it was only when Sandy tried to self-amputate his dying tail that we realized it had also been frost bitten. Surgery. Two months of a suppurating wound. Three types of antibiotics. And through it all, Sandy purred, full of affection, just happy to be alive.

It's strange that I patterned Lightning, a.k.a. Melancholy, a tailless cat, after one of my sister's cats, Put Put, gone many years ago, and that then one such creature drops into my life. Or should I say lap. Now Jackie, our other cat, has a rival. The lap is large, but not quite large enough for a big male ginger cat, tailless though he may be, and a little black girl cat at the same time. They've worked it out, though.

Mornings, when I write in the sunny living room, the lap belongs to Jackie. Evenings, when I doze in the cozy TV room, doing Sudoku and reading recipe books or bits of the paper, it belongs to Sandy. Or vice versa. And at night, Sandy warms my toes while Jackie warms my heart.

ABOUT THE AUTHOR

Born in Montreal and raised in Hudson, Quebec, Louise Carson studied music in Montreal and Toronto, played jazz piano and sang in the chorus of the Canadian Opera Company. Carson has published twelve books: *Rope: A Tale Told in Prose and Verse*, set in eighteenth-century Scotland; *Mermaid Road*, a lyrical novella; *A Clearing*, her first collection of poetry; *Executor*, a mystery set in China and Toronto; *In Which* and *Measured*: books one and two of her historical fantasy trilogy *The Chronicles of Deasil Widdy* (book three, *Third Circle*, is scheduled to appear in 2021); *Dog Poems*, her second collection of poetry; as well as the five Maples Mysteries: *The Cat Among Us, The Cat Vanishes, The Cat Between, The Cat Possessed* and now *A Clutter of Cats*.

Her poems appear in literary magazines, chapbooks and anthologies, including *The Best Canadian Poetry 2013* and *2021*. She's been shortlisted in *FreeFall* magazine's annual contest three times and won a Manitoba Magazine Award. Her novel *In Which* was shortlisted for a Quebec Writers' Federation prize in 2019. She has presented her work in many public forums in Montreal, Ottawa, Toronto, Saskatoon, Kingston and New York City.

With her adult daughter and three pets, she lives in St-Lazare, Quebec, where she writes, teaches music and gardens.